1-GRAPHIC NOVELS

P9-DFR-572

ORILLIA PUBLIC LIBRARY
FEB 18 2011
CHILDREN'S DEPARTMENT

A SAM & FRIENDS MYSTERY

BOOK THREE

Mummy Mayhem

MARY LABATT • JO RIOUX

KIDS CAN PRESS

Labatt, M.
Mummy mayhem.

PRICE: $7.95

JAN 2011

Text © 2010 Mary Labatt
Illustrations © 2010 Jo Rioux

All rights reserved. No part of this publication may be reproduced, stored in a retrieval system or transmitted, in any form or by any means, without the prior written permission of Kids Can Press Ltd. or, in case of photocopying or other reprographic copying, a license from The Canadian Copyright Licensing Agency (Access Copyright). For an Access Copyright license, visit www.accesscopyright.ca or call toll free to 1-800-893-5777.

This is a work of fiction and any resemblance of characters to persons living or dead is purely coincidental.

Kids Can Press acknowledges the financial support of the Government of Ontario, through the Ontario Media Development Corporation's Ontario Book Initiative; the Ontario Arts Council; the Canada Council for the Arts; and the Government of Canada, through the BPIDP, for our publishing activity.

Published in Canada by
Kids Can Press Ltd.
29 Birch Avenue
Toronto, ON M4V 1E2

Published in the U.S. by
Kids Can Press Ltd.
2250 Military Road
Tonawanda, NY 14150

www.kidscanpress.com

Based on the book *The Mummy Lives!* by Mary Labatt.

Edited by Karen Li
Designed by Kathleen Gray

Manufactured in Buji, Shenzhen, China, in 3/2010 by WKT Company

CM 10 0 9 8 7 6 5 4 3 2 1
CM PA 10 0 9 8 7 6 5 4 3 2 1

Library and Archives Canada Cataloguing in Publication

Labatt, Mary, 1944–
Mummy mayhem / Mary Labatt ; illustrated by Jo Rioux.

(A Sam & friends mystery bk. 3)
ISBN 978-1-55453-470-8 (bound). ISBN 978-1-55453-471-5 (pbk.)

I. Rioux, Jo-Anne II. Title. III. Series.

PS8573.A135M86 2010   jC813'.54   C2010-900107-9

Kids Can Press is a *corus*™ Entertainment company

To my family — M.L.
To Keith — J.R.

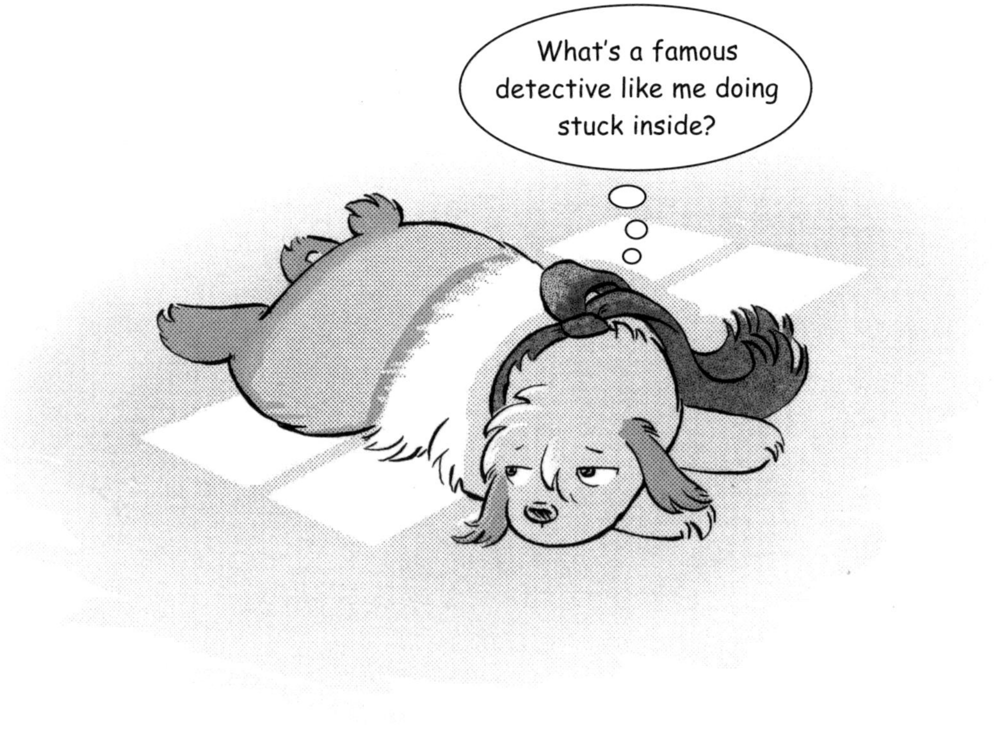
What's a famous detective like me doing stuck inside?

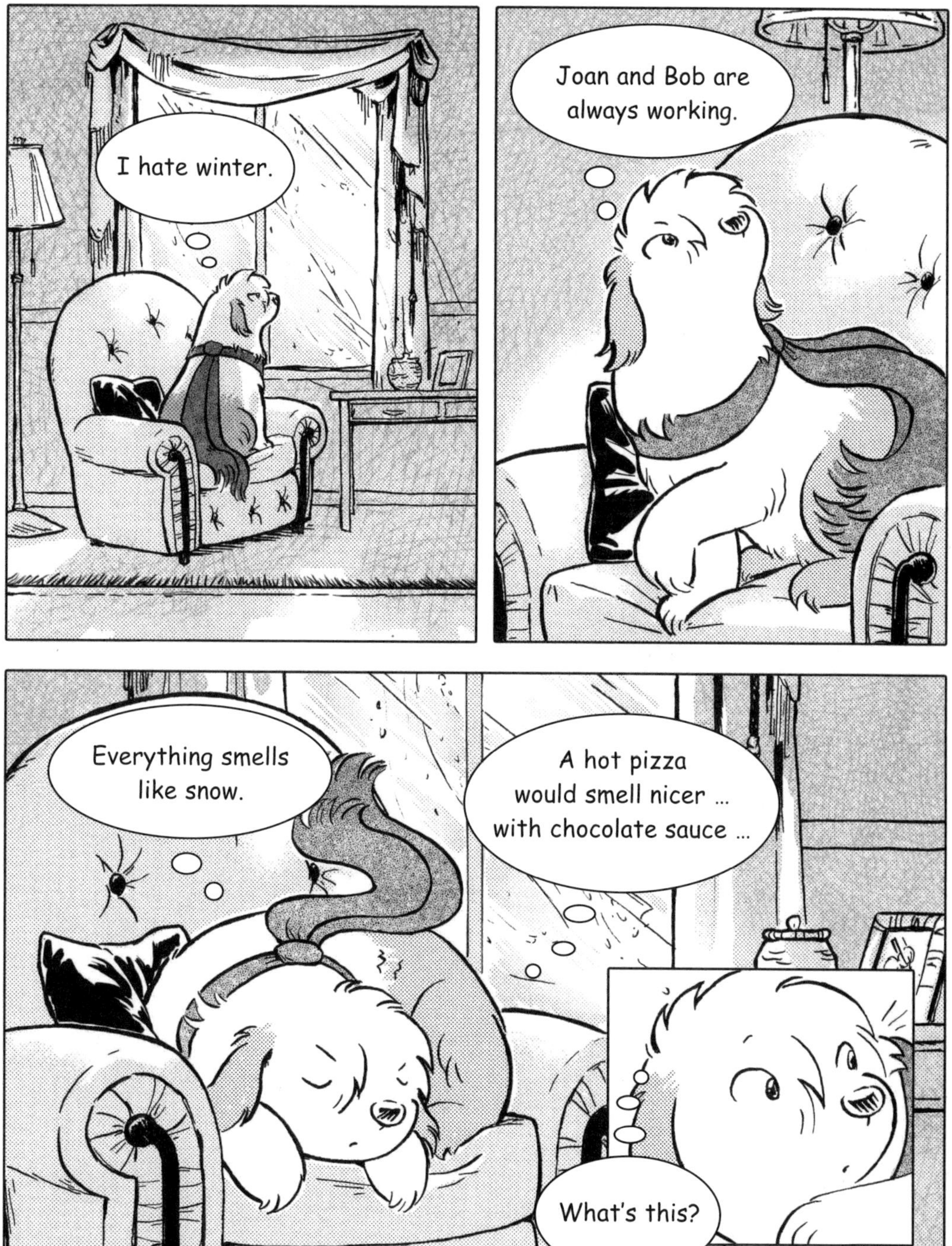
I hate winter.
Joan and Bob are always working.
Everything smells like snow.
A hot pizza would smell nicer ... with chocolate sauce ...
What's this?

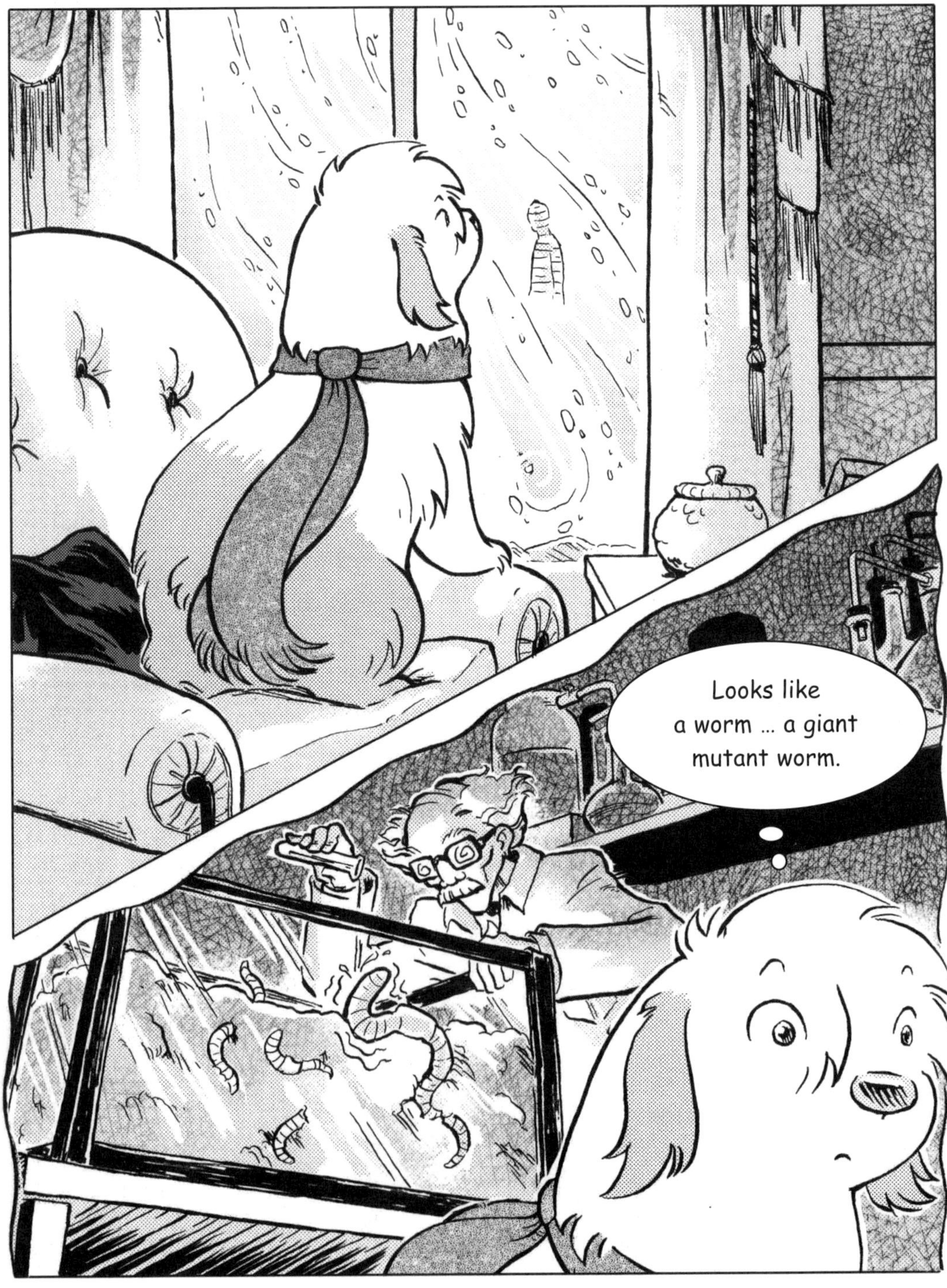
Looks like a worm ... a giant mutant worm.

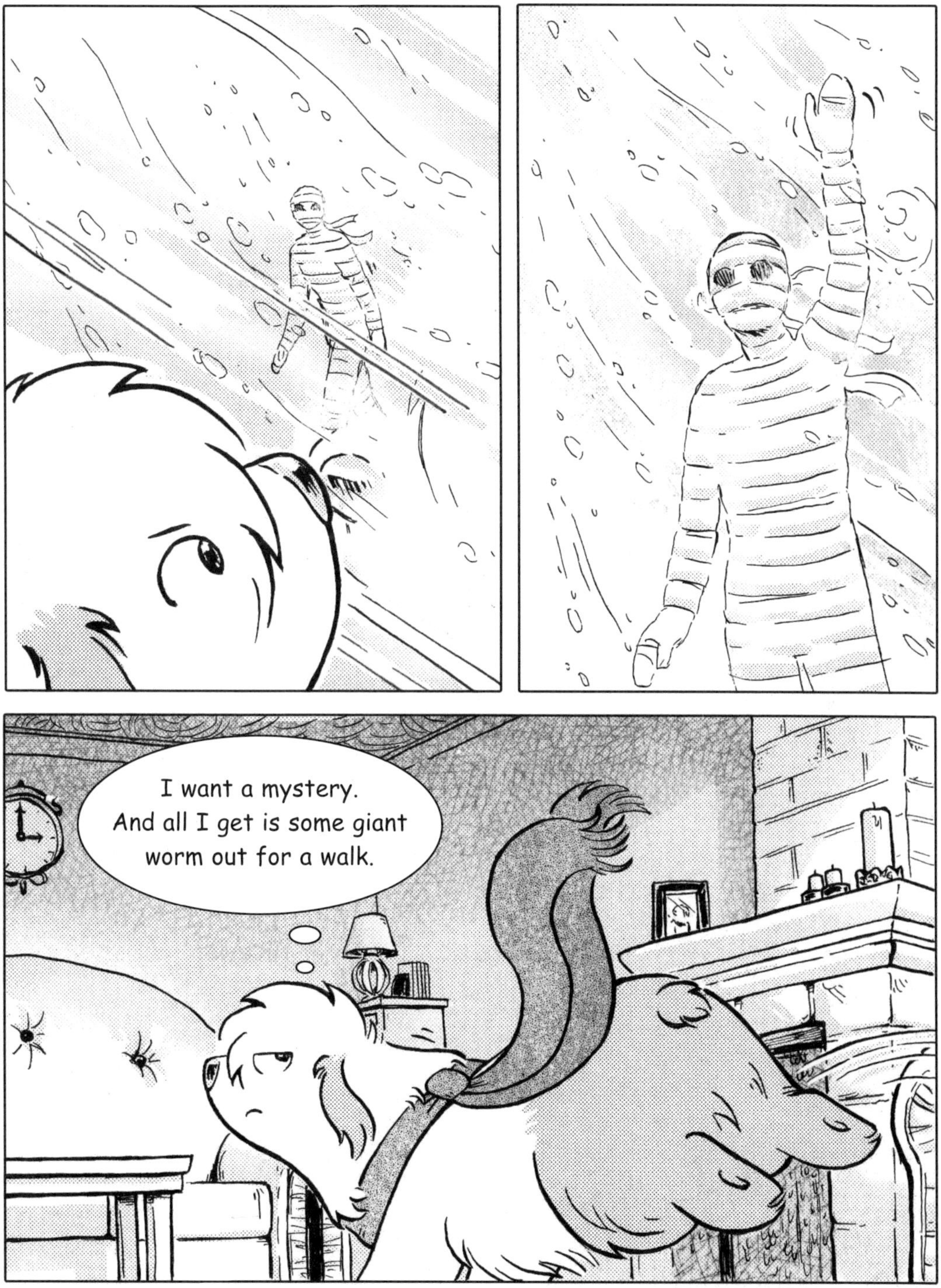
I want a mystery.
And all I get is some giant
worm out for a walk.

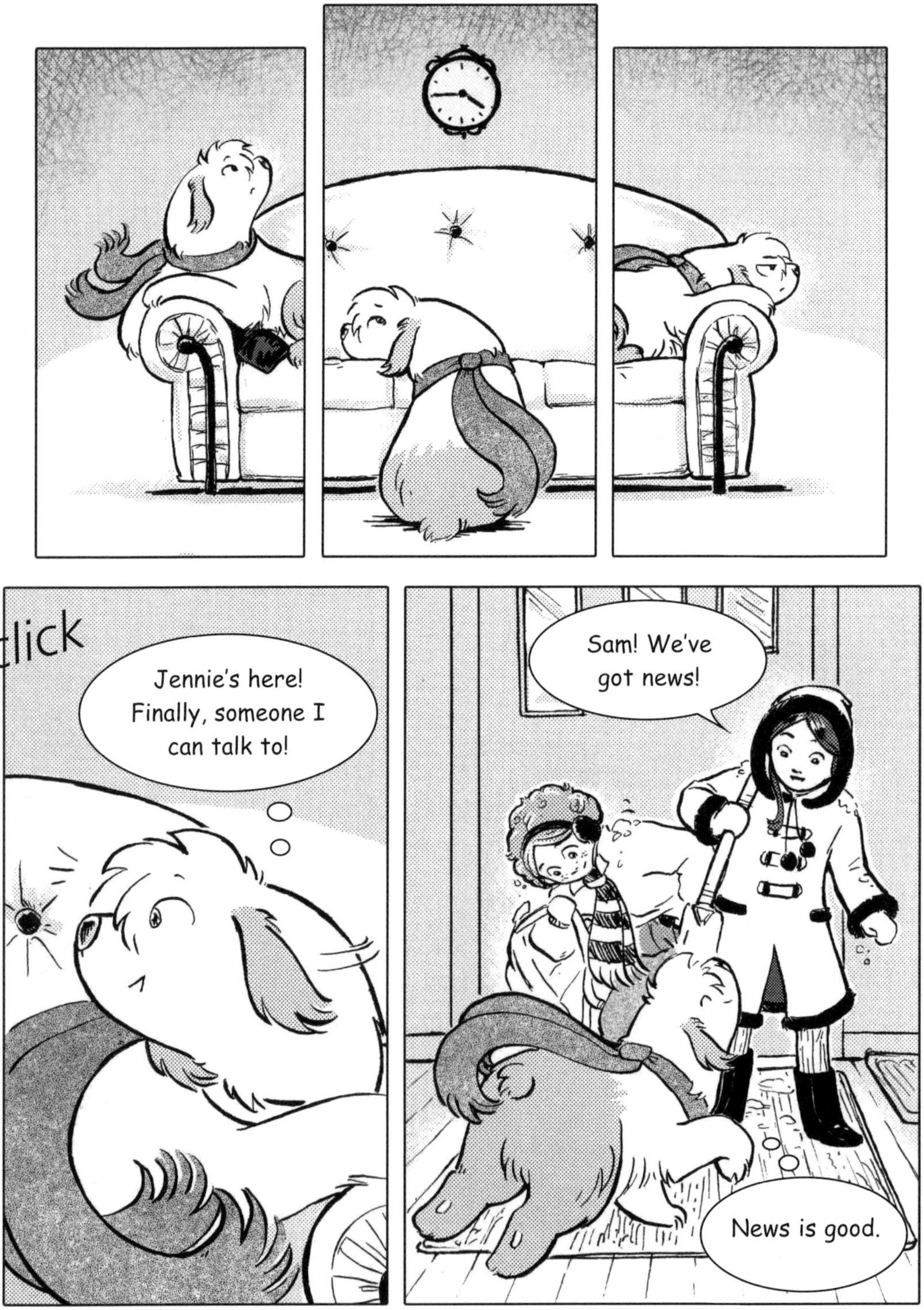
click
Jennie's here! Finally, someone I can talk to!
Sam! We've got news!
News is good.

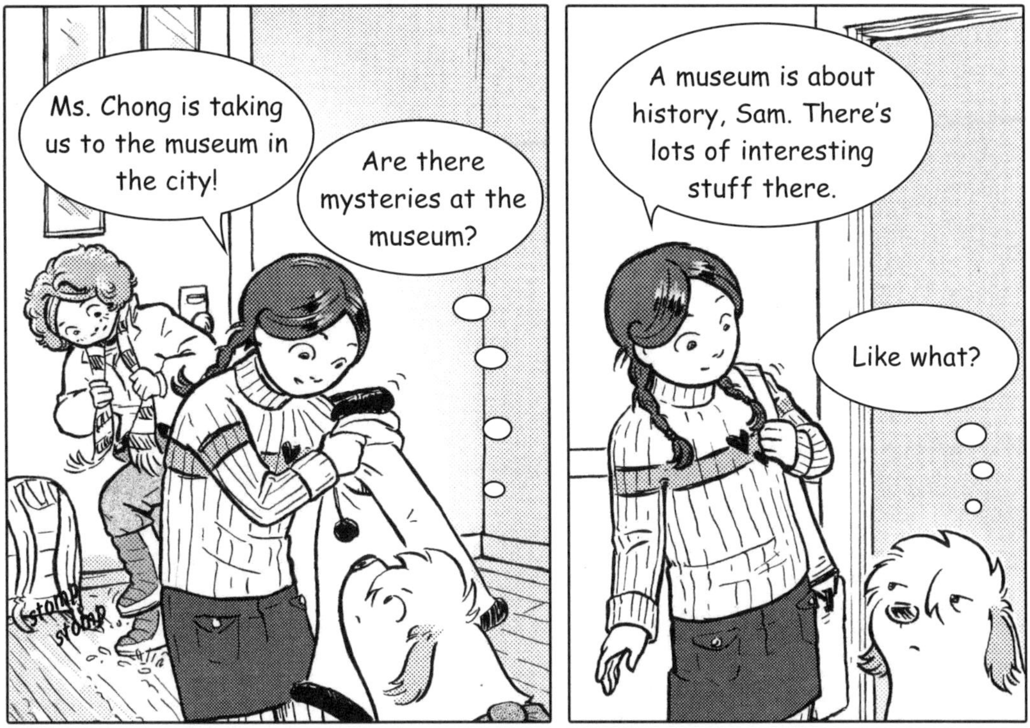
Ms. Chong is taking us to the museum in the city!
stomp
stomp
Are there mysteries at the museum?
A museum is about history, Sam. There's lots of interesting stuff there.
Like what?

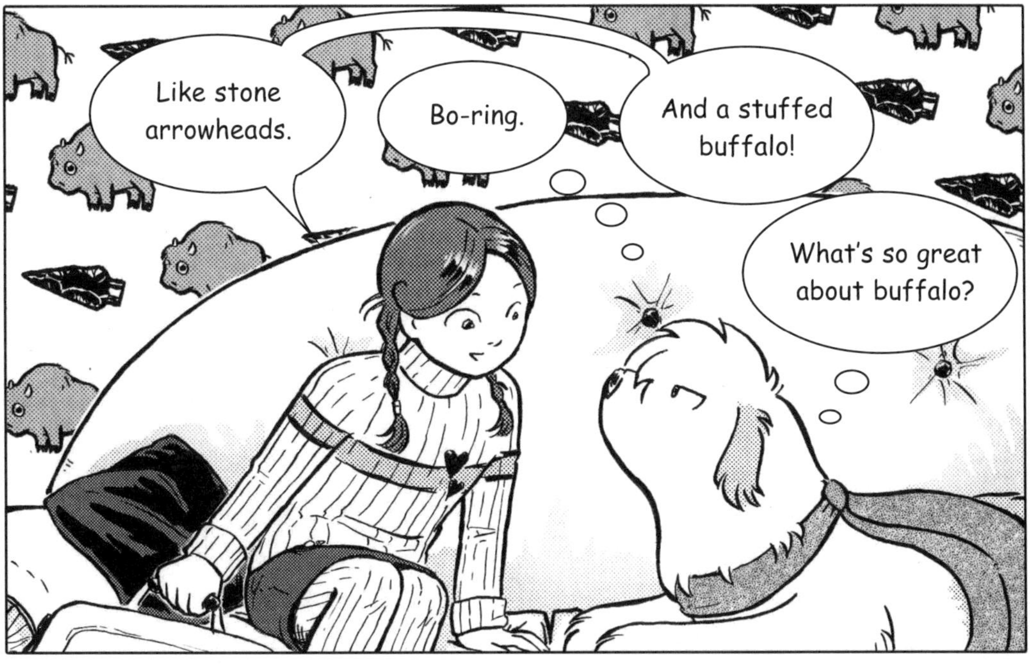
Like stone arrowheads.
Bo-ring.
And a stuffed buffalo!
What's so great about buffalo?

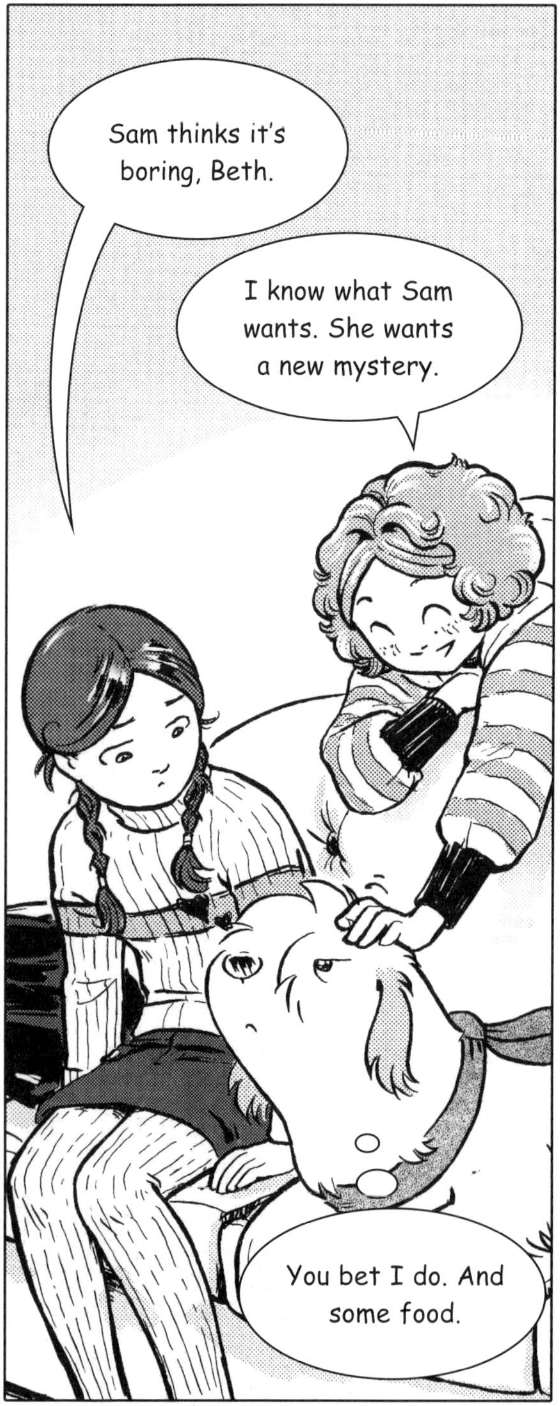
Sam thinks it's boring, Beth.
I know what Sam wants. She wants a new mystery.
You bet I do. And some food.

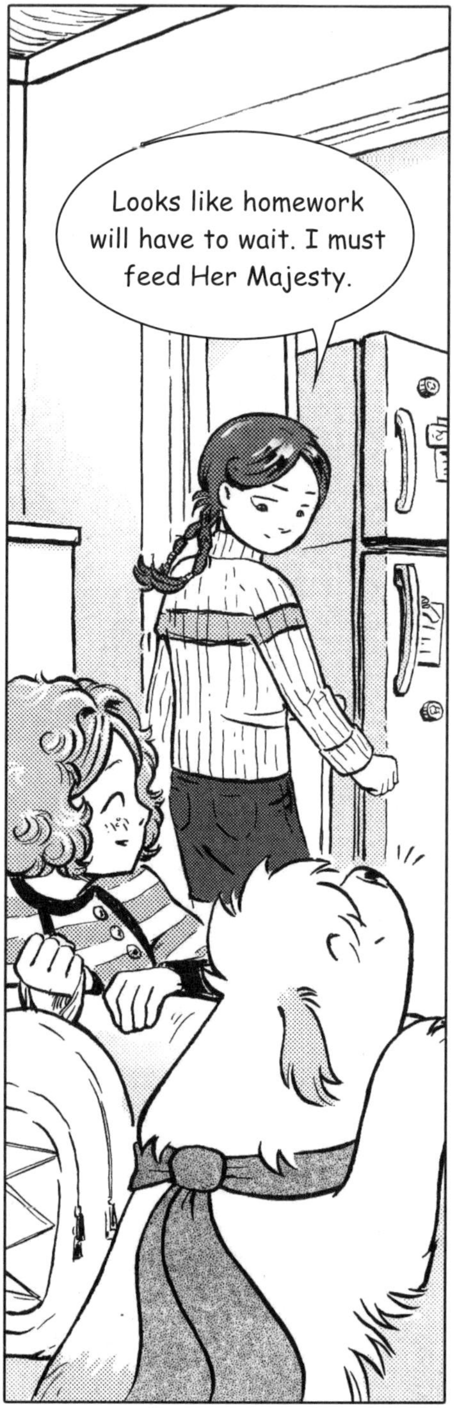
Looks like homework will have to wait. I must feed Her Majesty.

Later ...
Ms. Chong says we can choose our favorite part of the museum for our research project.
I like arrowheads a lot ...
Who cares about arrowheads? What we need is a mystery.
I'm going to do my project on Egypt. Ms. Chong said there's a mummy in the museum.

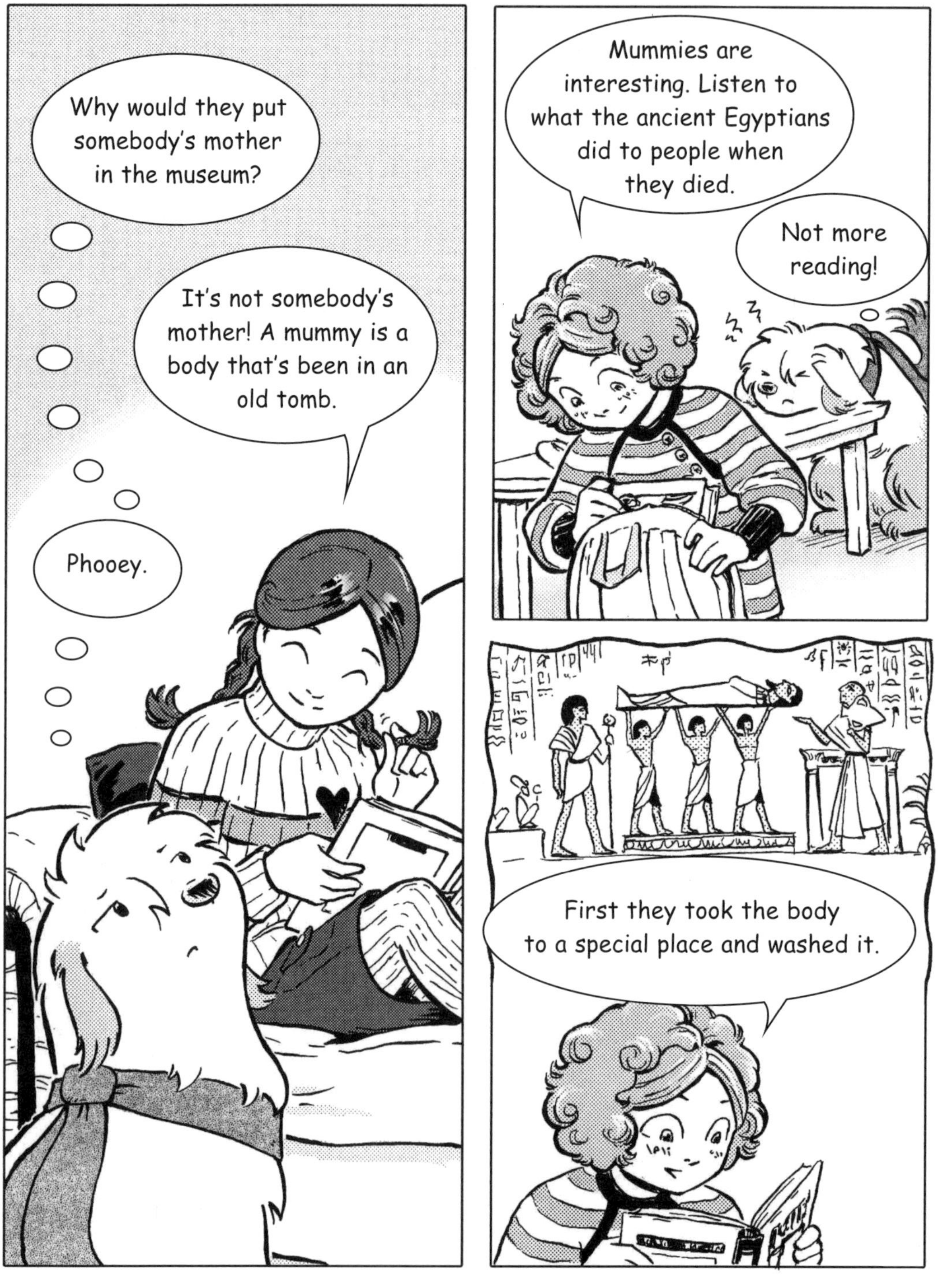
Why would they put somebody's mother in the museum?
It's not somebody's mother! A mummy is a body that's been in an old tomb.
Phooey.
Mummies are interesting. Listen to what the ancient Egyptians did to people when they died.
Not more reading!
First they took the body to a special place and washed it.

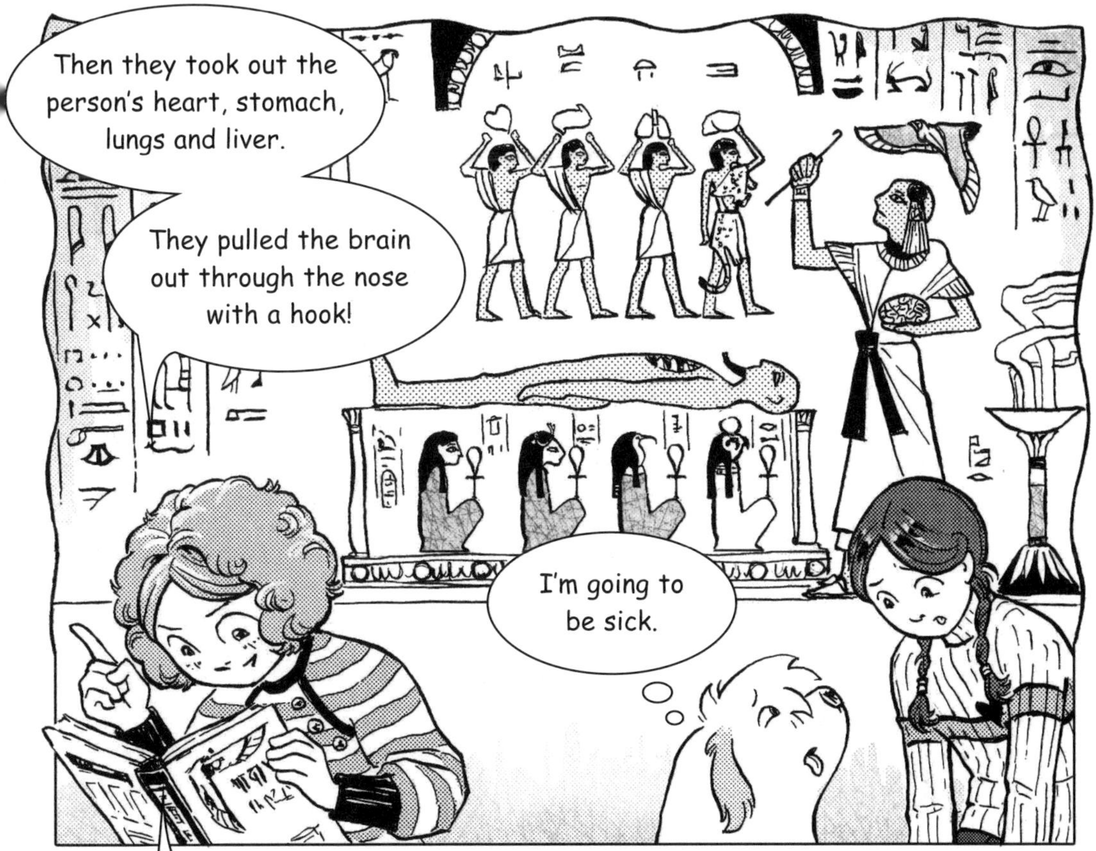
Then they took out the person's heart, stomach, lungs and liver.
They pulled the brain out through the nose with a hook!
I'm going to be sick.

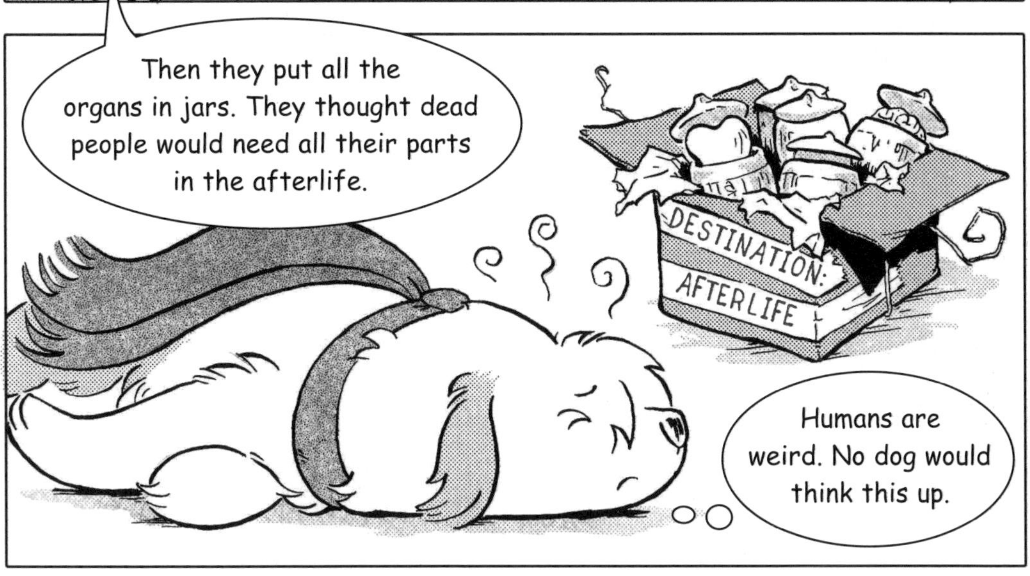
Then they put all the organs in jars. They thought dead people would need all their parts in the afterlife.
DESTINATION: AFTERLIFE
Humans are weird. No dog would think this up.

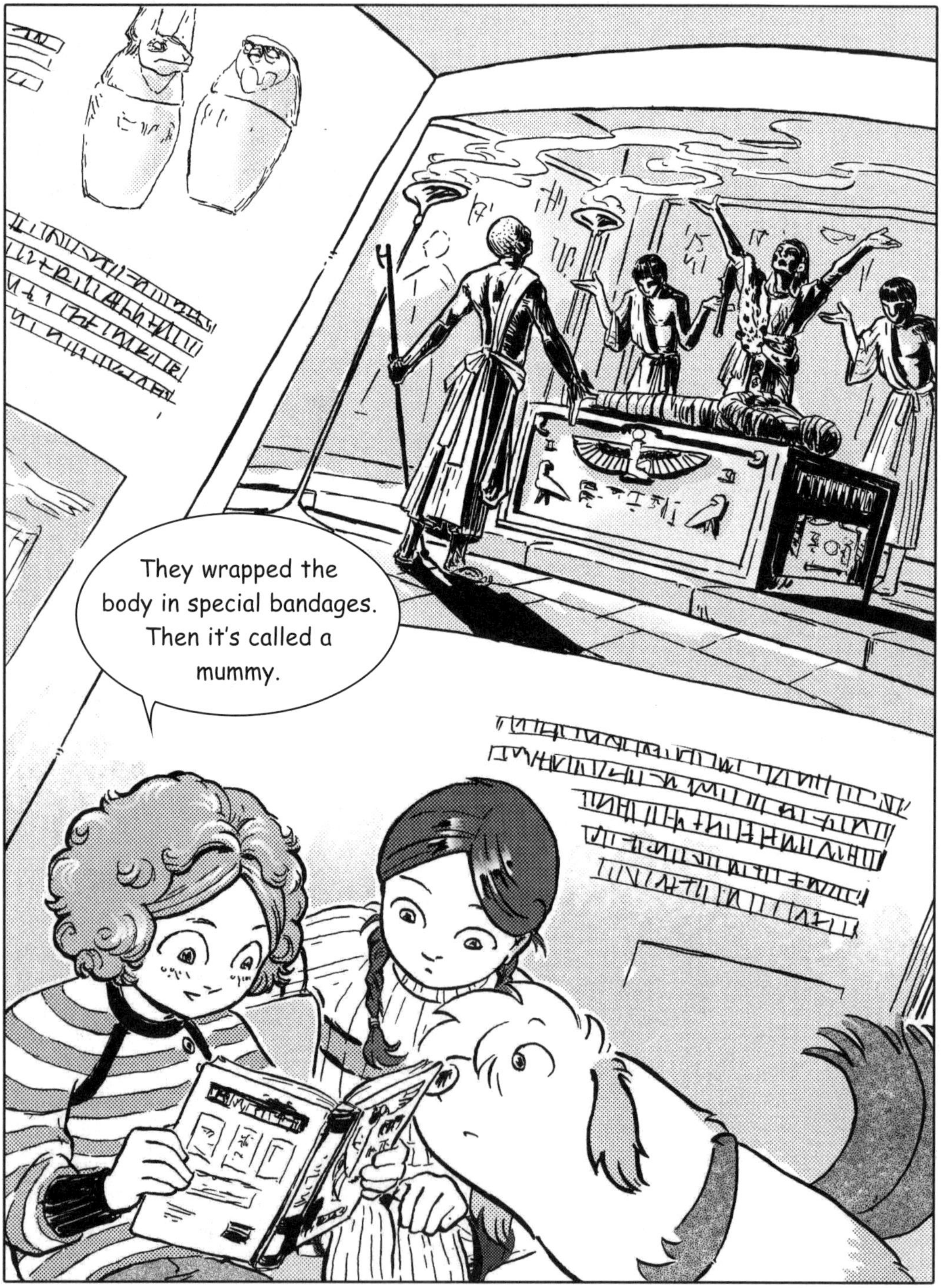
They wrapped the body in special bandages. Then it's called a mummy.

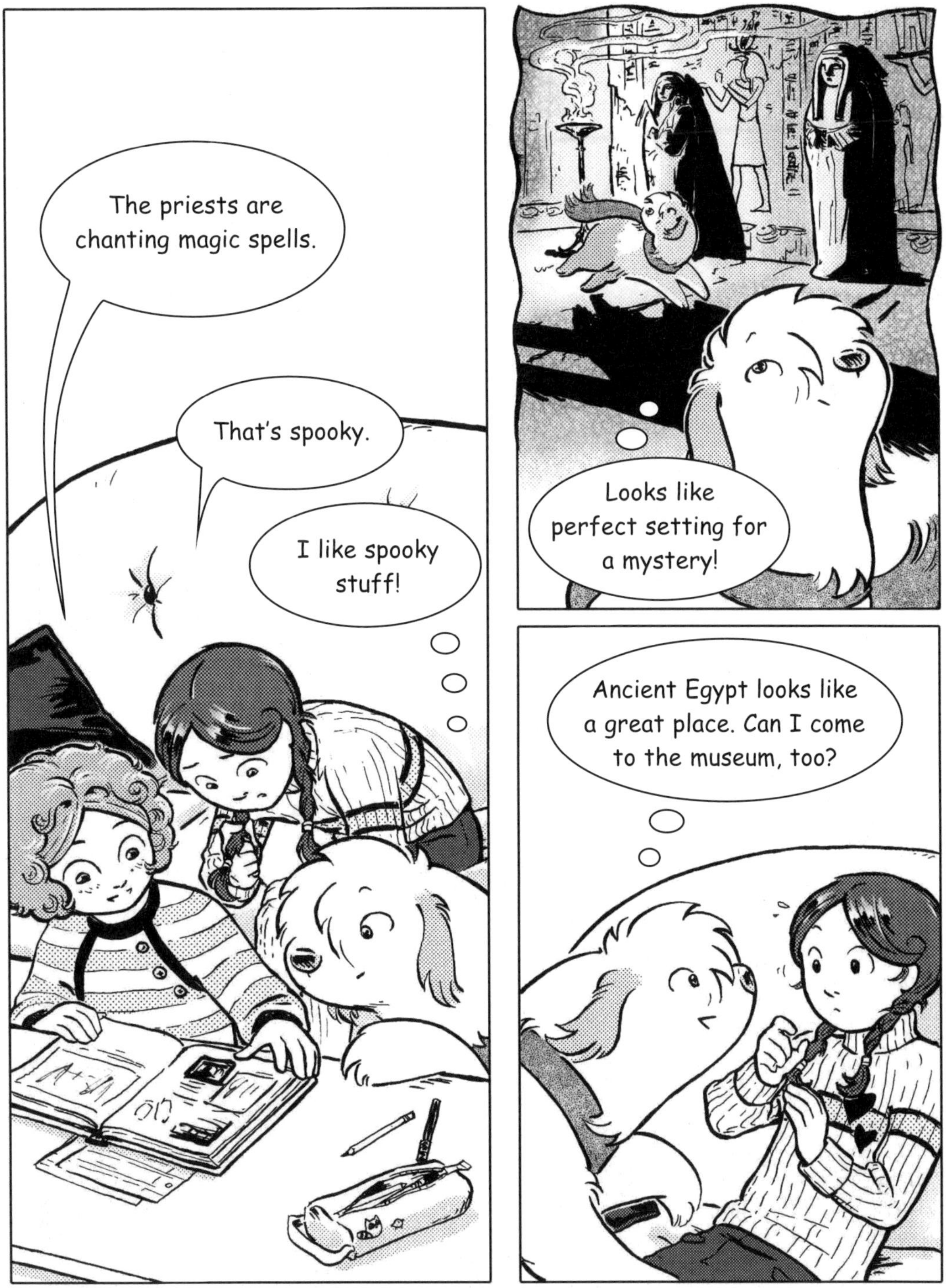
The priests are chanting magic spells.
That's spooky.
I like spooky stuff!
Looks like perfect setting for a mystery!
Ancient Egypt looks like a great place. Can I come to the museum, too?

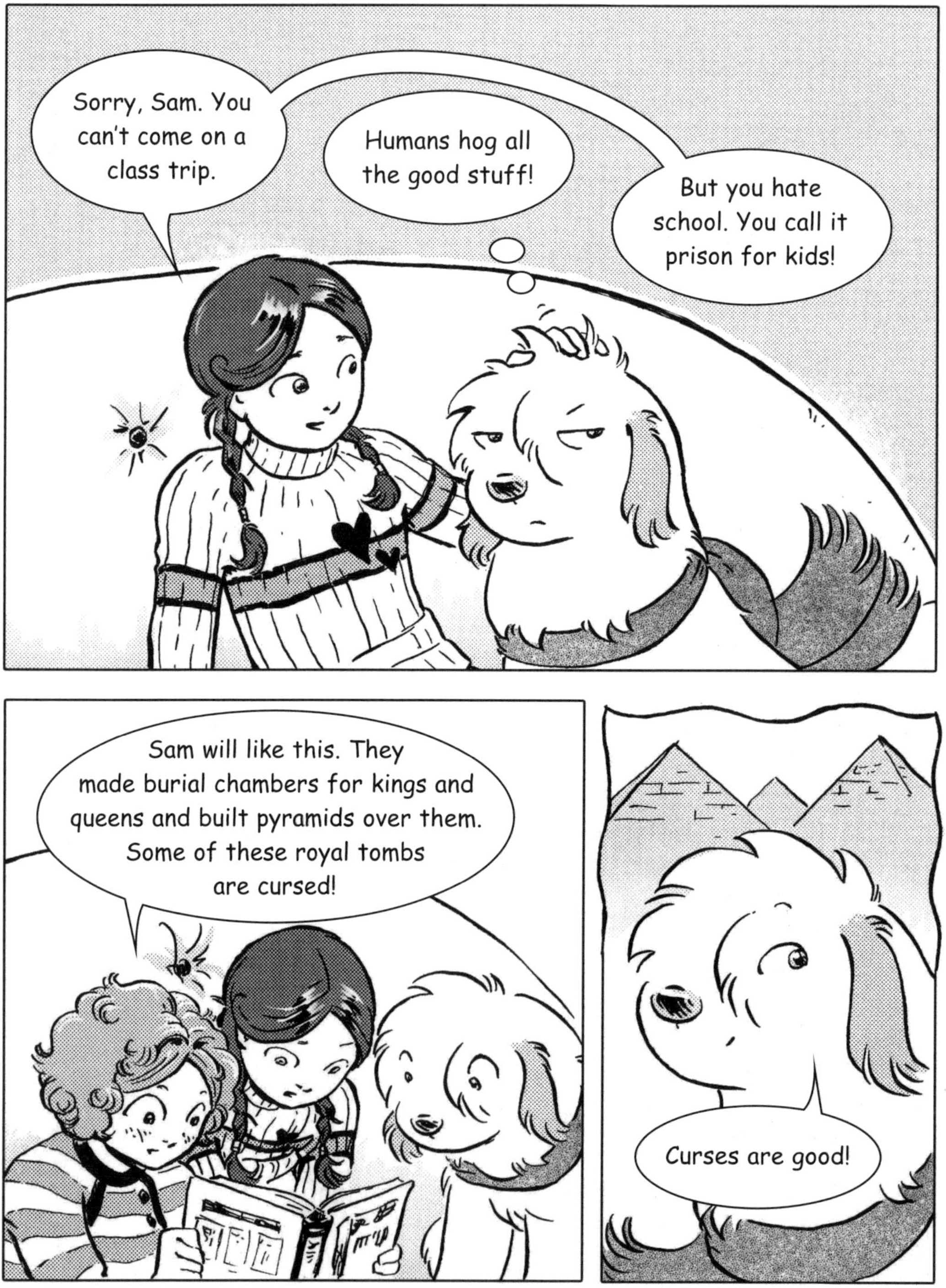
Sorry, Sam. You can't come on a class trip.
Humans hog all the good stuff!
But you hate school. You call it prison for kids!
Sam will like this. They made burial chambers for kings and queens and built pyramids over them. Some of these royal tombs are cursed!
Curses are good!

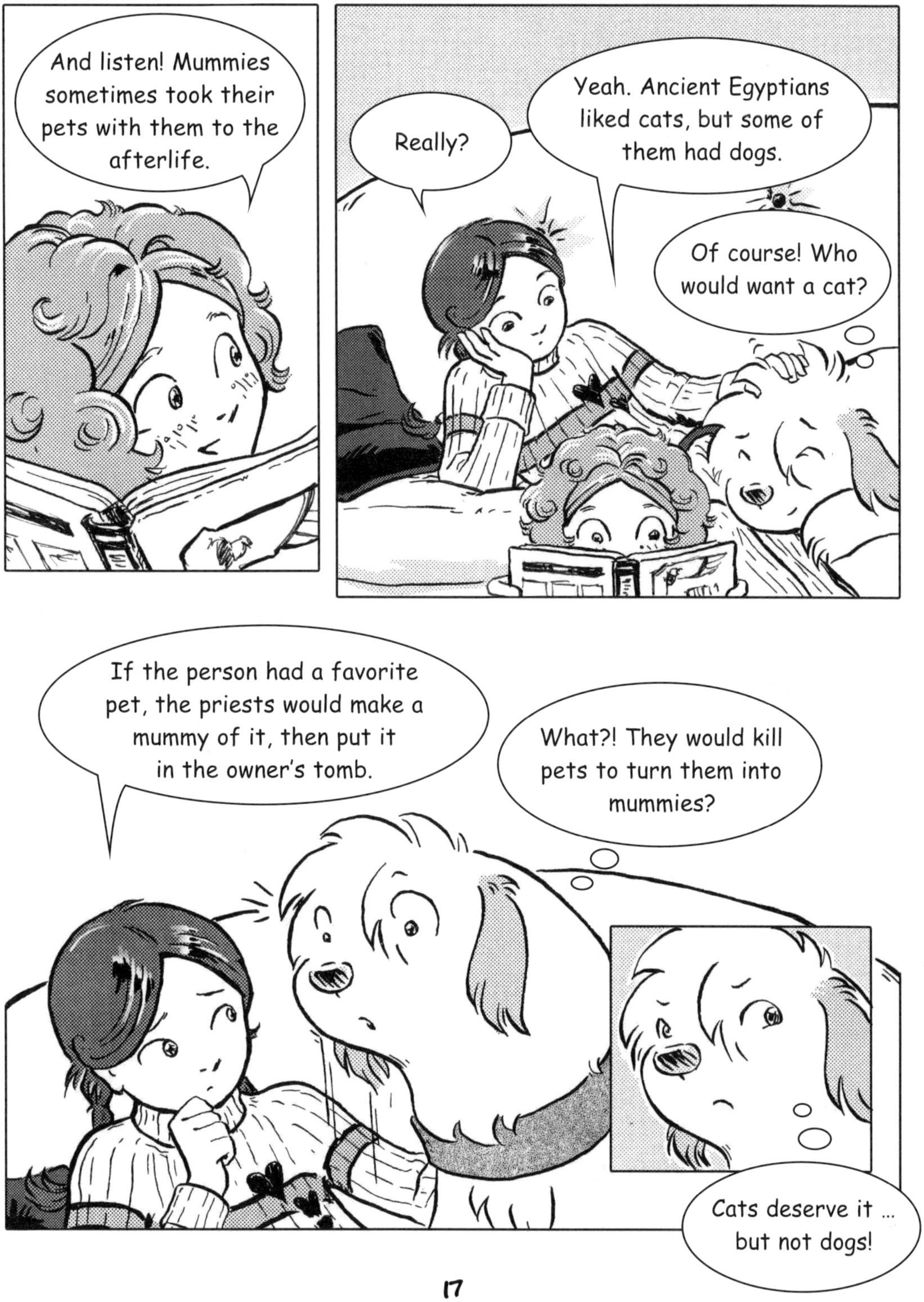
And listen! Mummies sometimes took their pets with them to the afterlife.
Really?
Yeah. Ancient Egyptians liked cats, but some of them had dogs.
Of course! Who would want a cat?
If the person had a favorite pet, the priests would make a mummy of it, then put it in the owner's tomb.
What?! They would kill pets to turn them into mummies?
Cats deserve it … but not dogs!

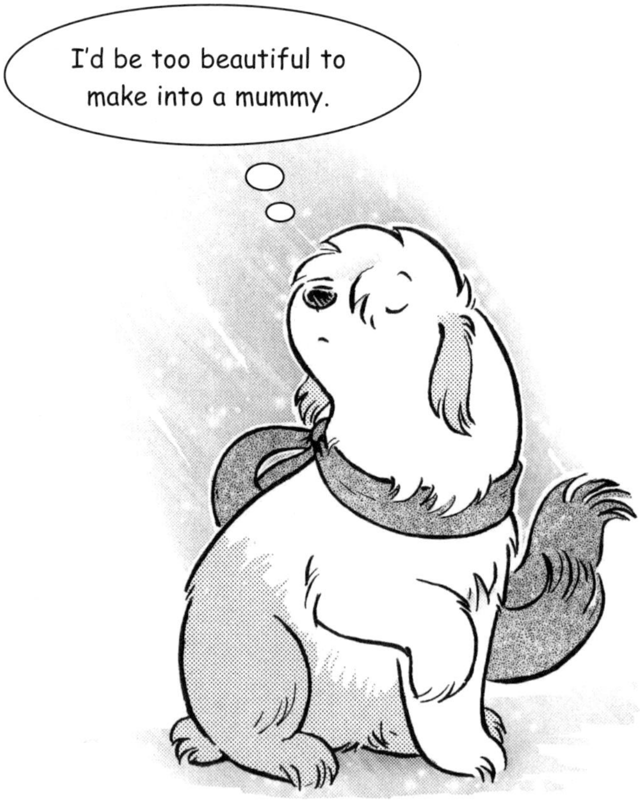
I'd be too beautiful to make into a mummy.

The next week ...

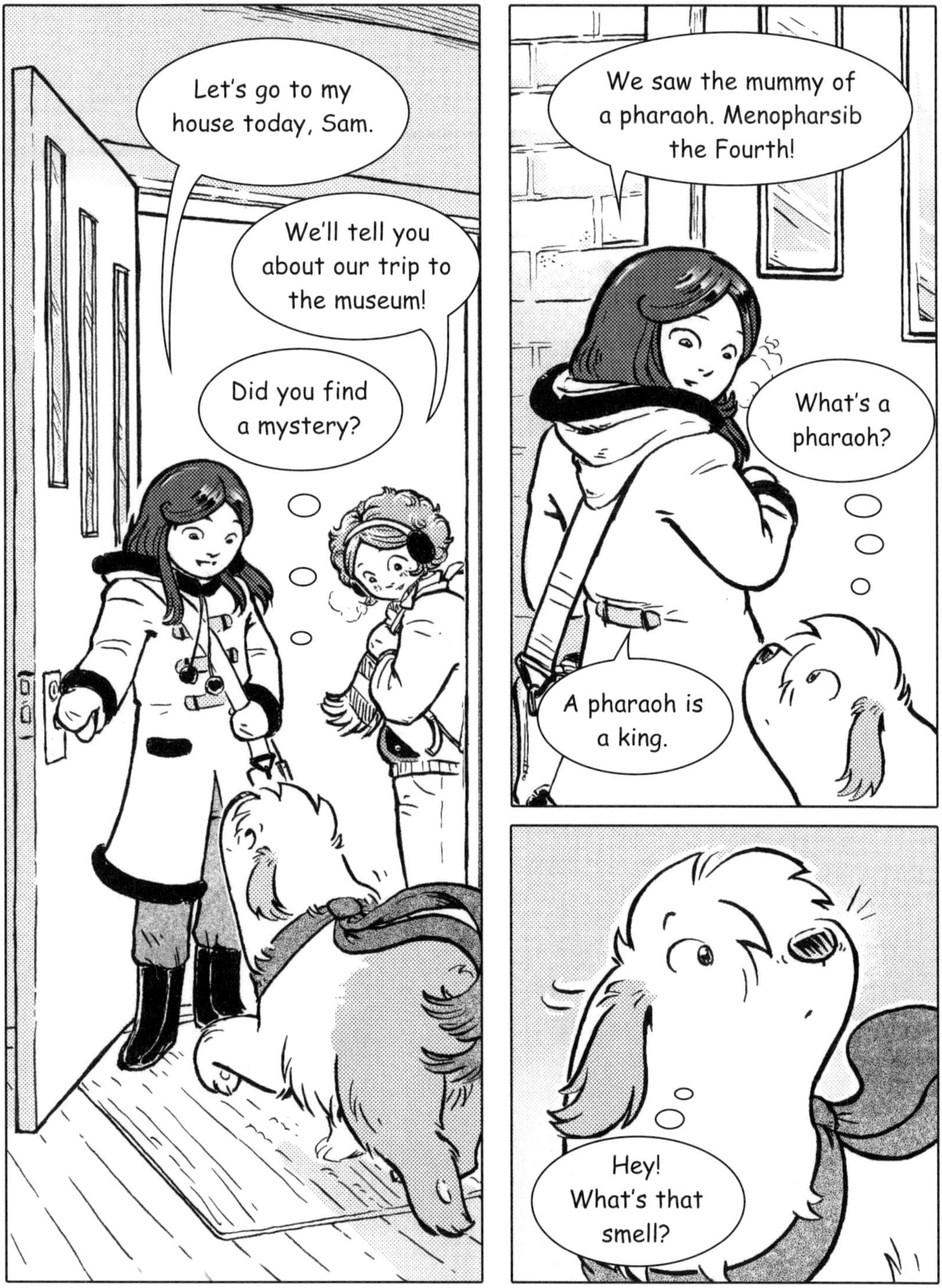
Let's go to my house today, Sam.
We'll tell you about our trip to the museum!
Did you find a mystery?
We saw the mummy of a pharaoh. Menopharsib the Fourth!
What's a pharaoh?
A pharaoh is a king.
Hey! What's that smell?

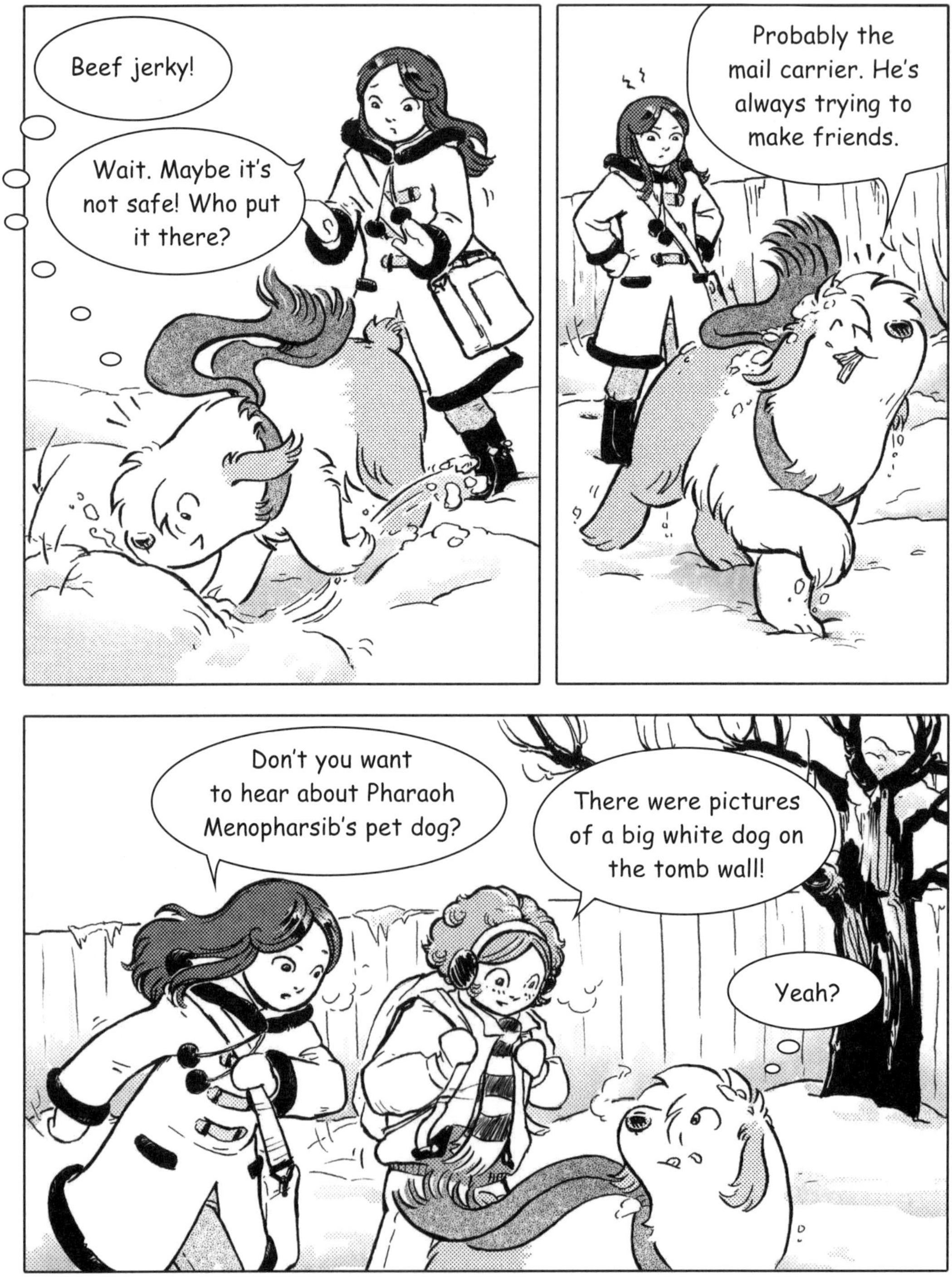
Beef jerky!
Wait. Maybe it's not safe! Who put it there?
Probably the mail carrier. He's always trying to make friends.
Don't you want to hear about Pharaoh Menopharsib's pet dog?
There were pictures of a big white dog on the tomb wall!
Yeah?

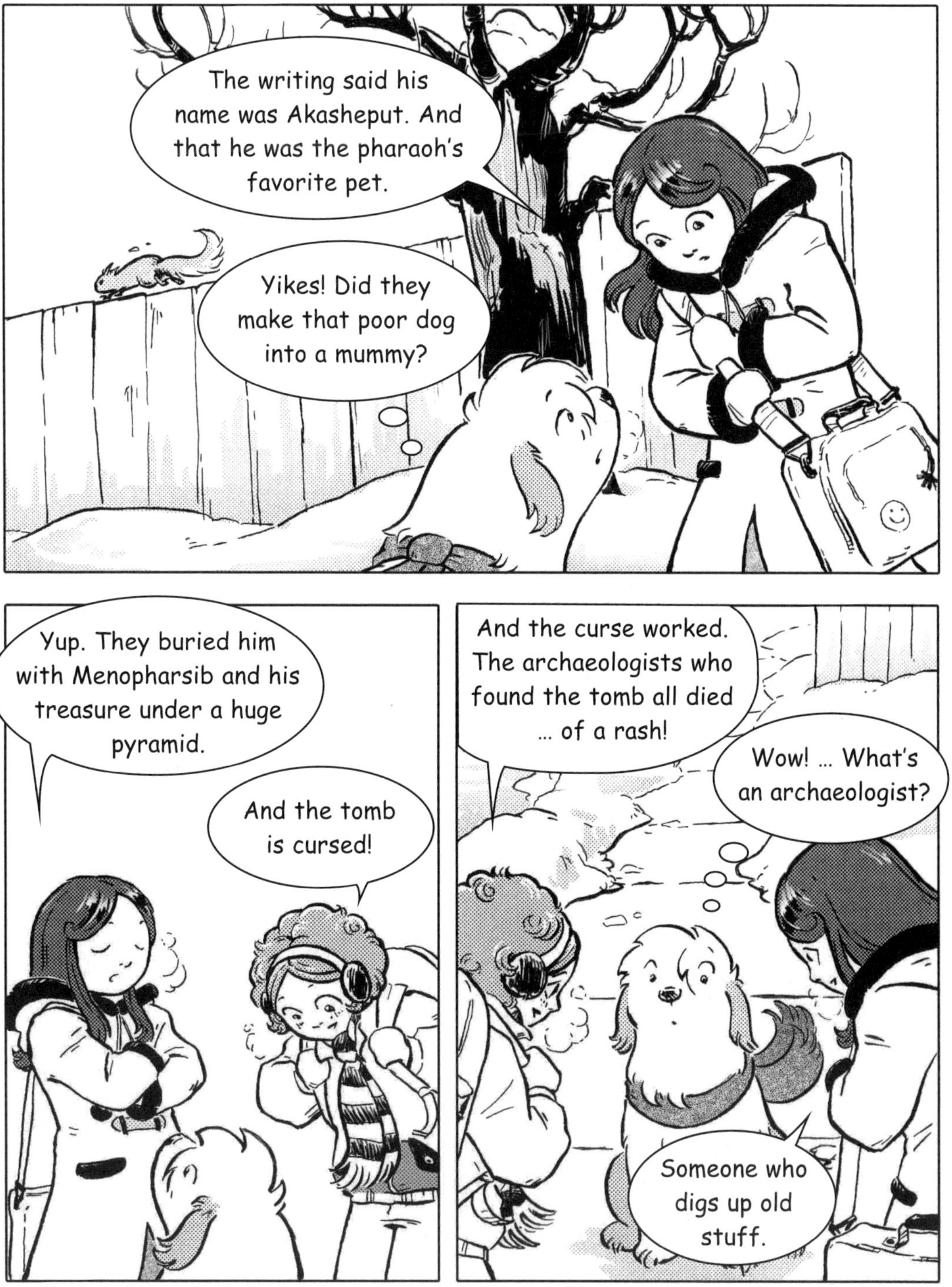
The writing said his name was Akasheput. And that he was the pharaoh's favorite pet.
Yikes! Did they make that poor dog into a mummy?
Yup. They buried him with Menopharsib and his treasure under a huge pyramid.
And the tomb is cursed!
And the curse worked. The archaeologists who found the tomb all died ... of a rash!
Wow! ... What's an archaeologist?
Someone who digs up old stuff.

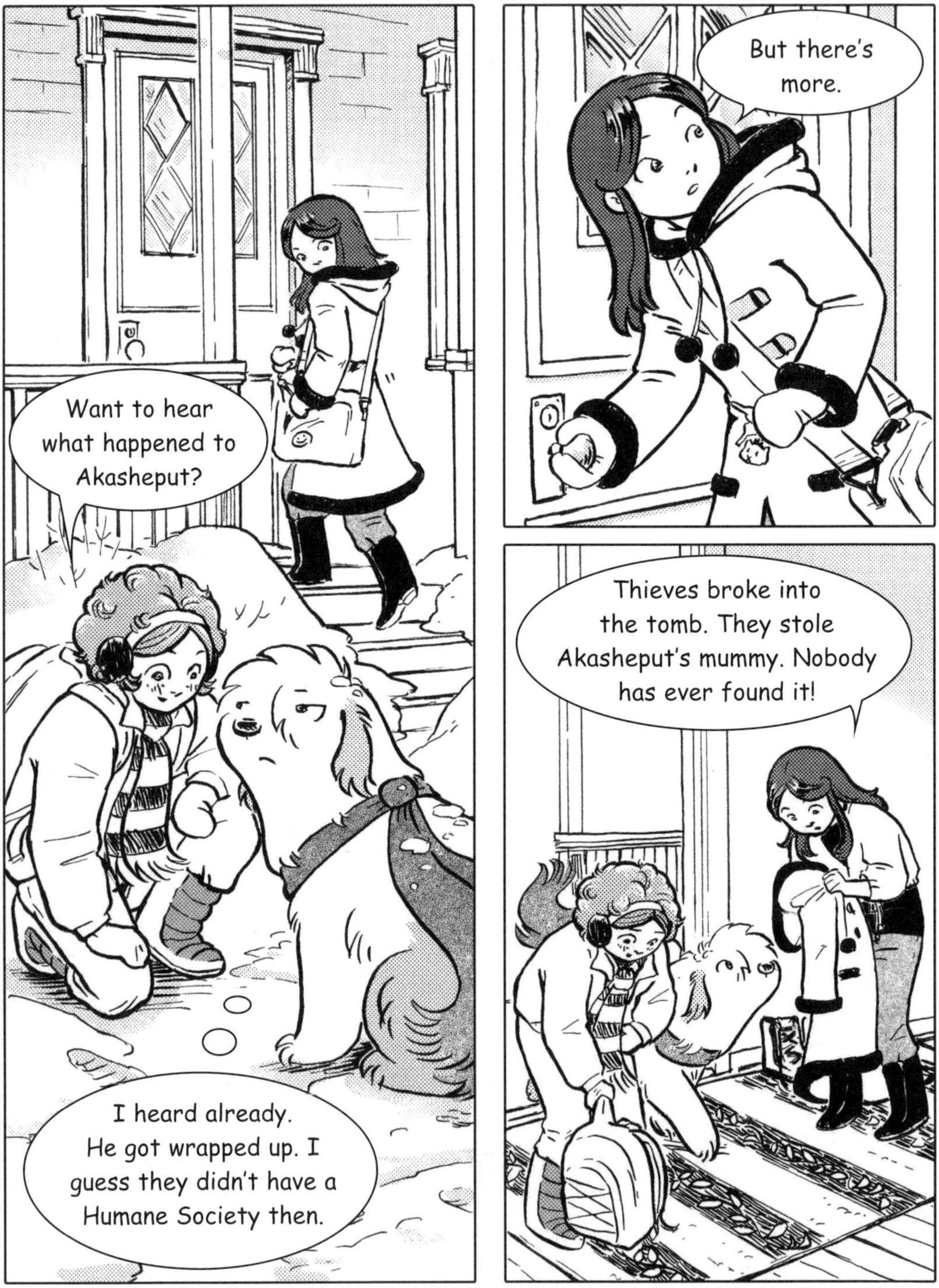

Want to hear what happened to Akasheput?
I heard already. He got wrapped up. I guess they didn't have a Humane Society then.
But there's more.
Thieves broke into the tomb. They stole Akasheput's mummy. Nobody has ever found it!

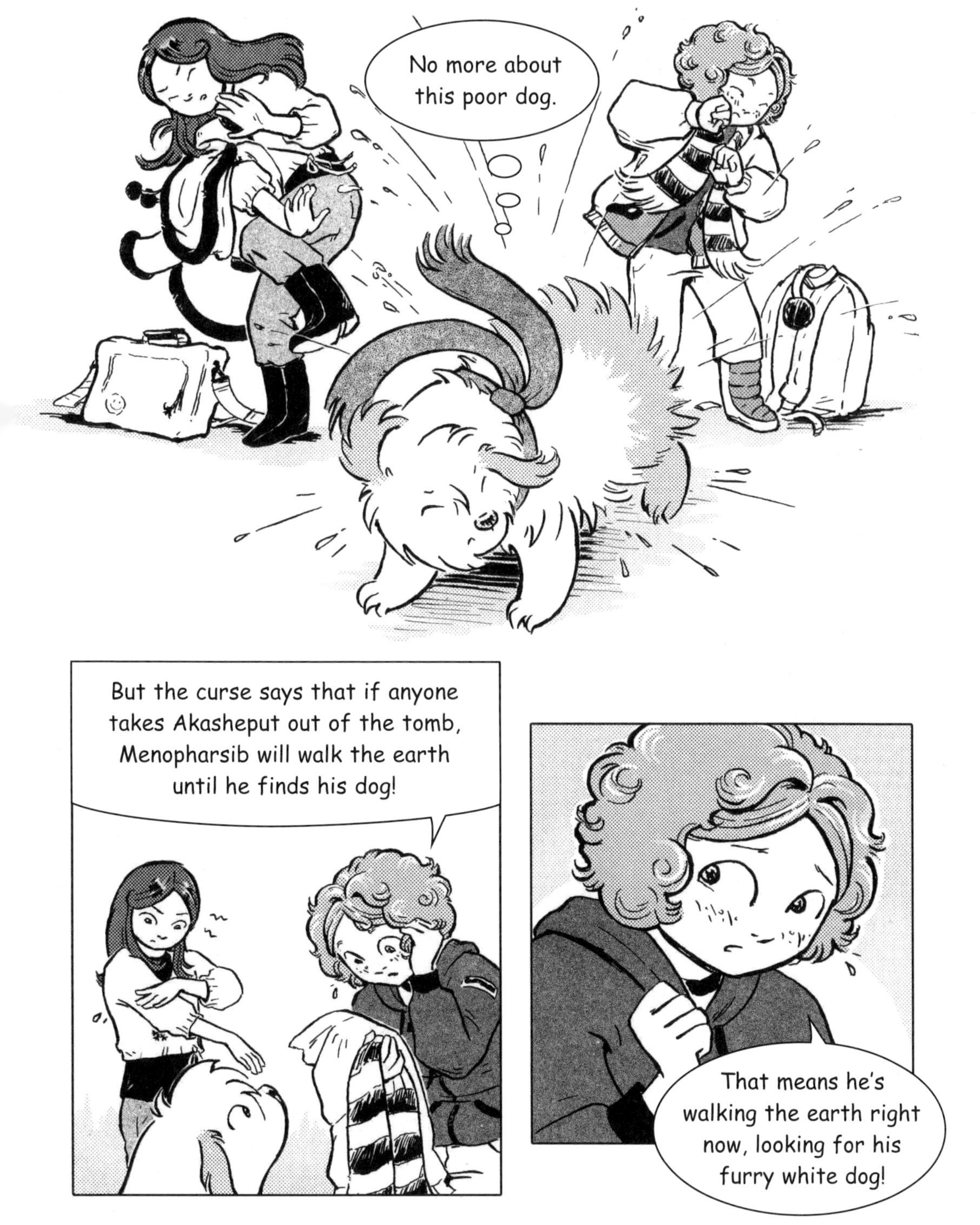
No more about this poor dog.
But the curse says that if anyone takes Akasheput out of the tomb, Menopharsib will walk the earth until he finds his dog!
That means he's walking the earth right now, looking for his furry white dog!

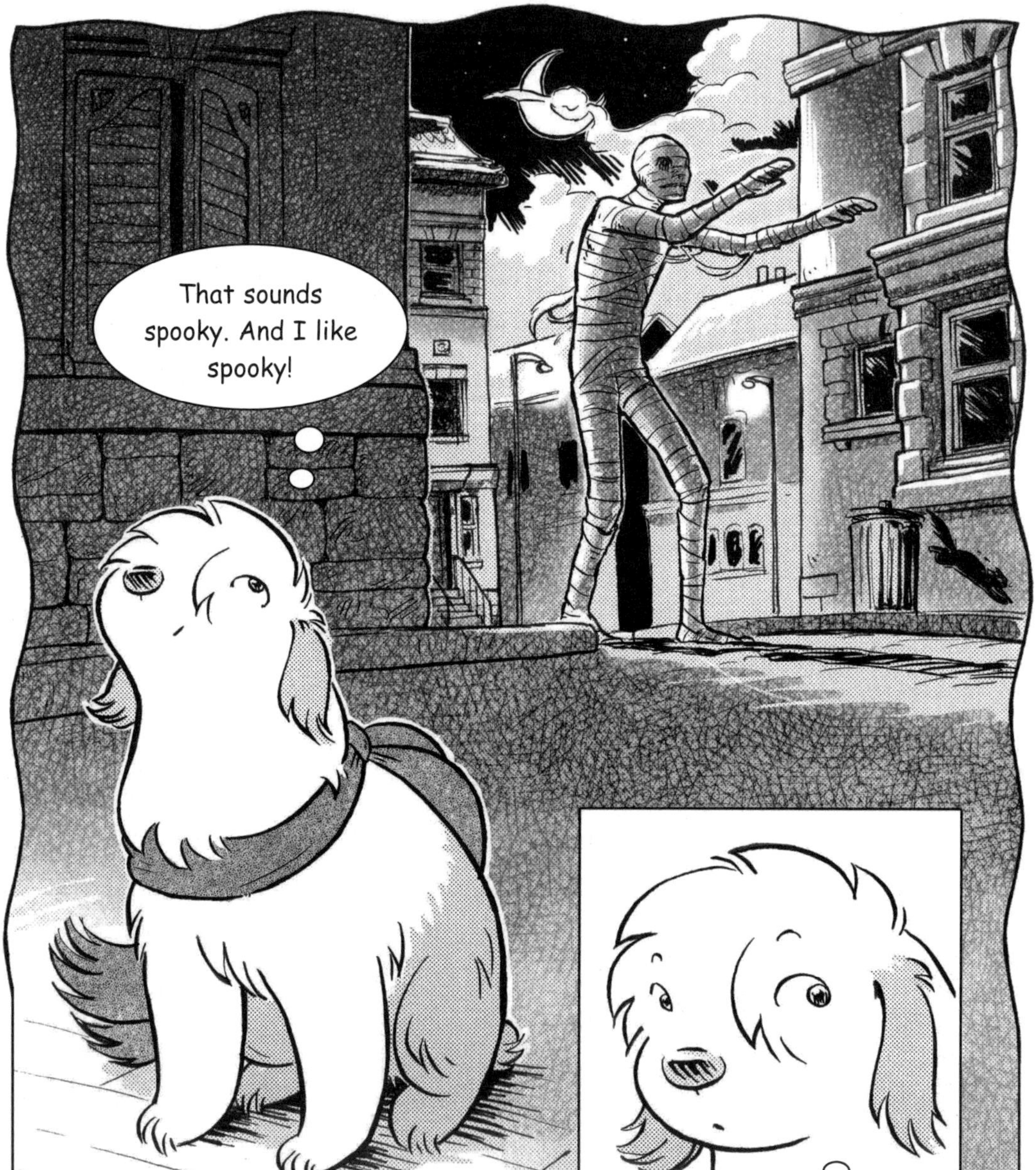
That sounds spooky. And I like spooky!
Hey! *I'm* big and white and furry. I hope he doesn't come after me.

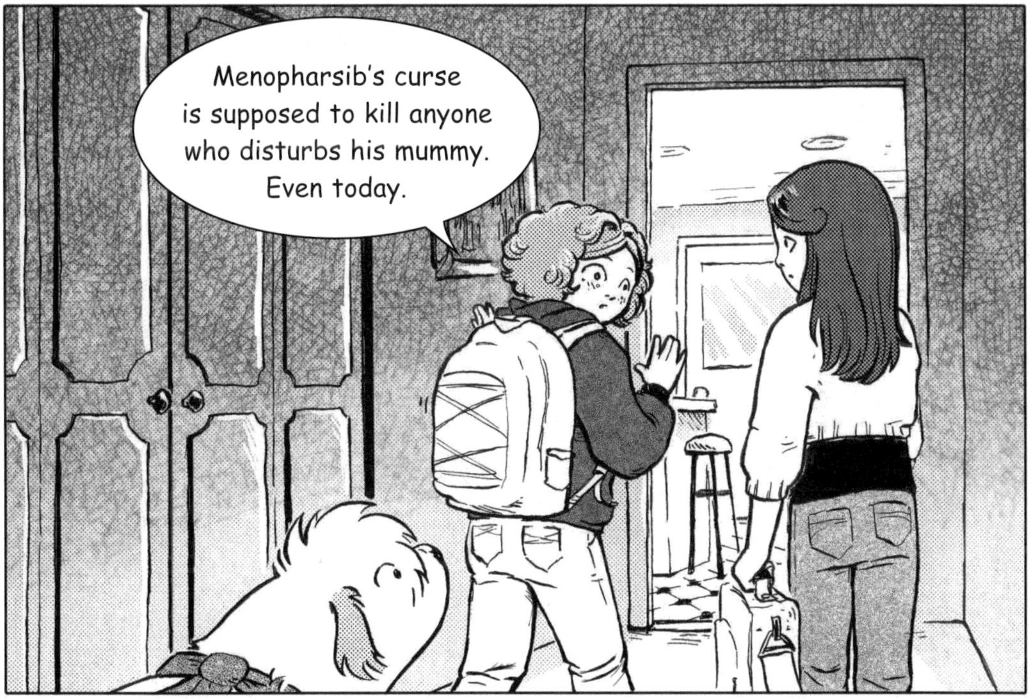
Menopharsib's curse is supposed to kill anyone who disturbs his mummy. Even today.

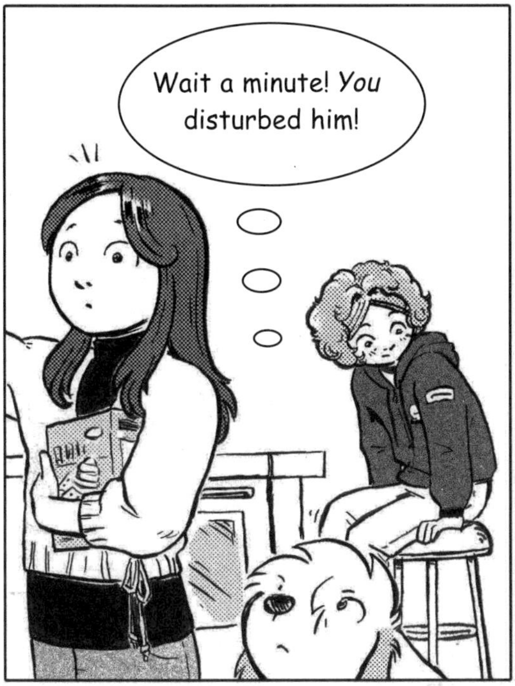
Wait a minute! *You* disturbed him!

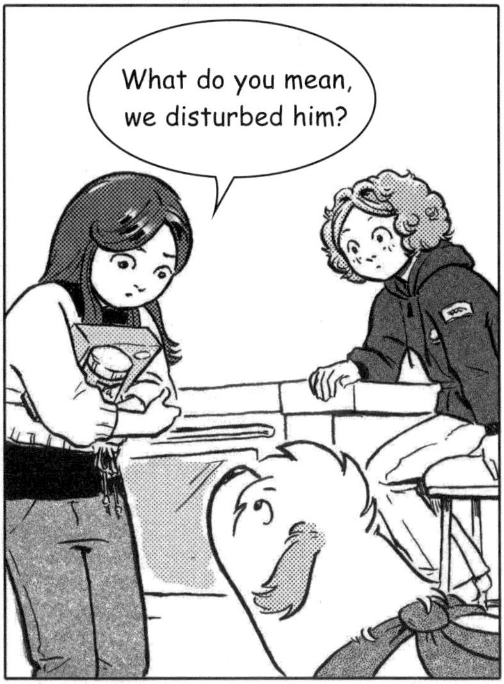
What do you mean, we disturbed him?

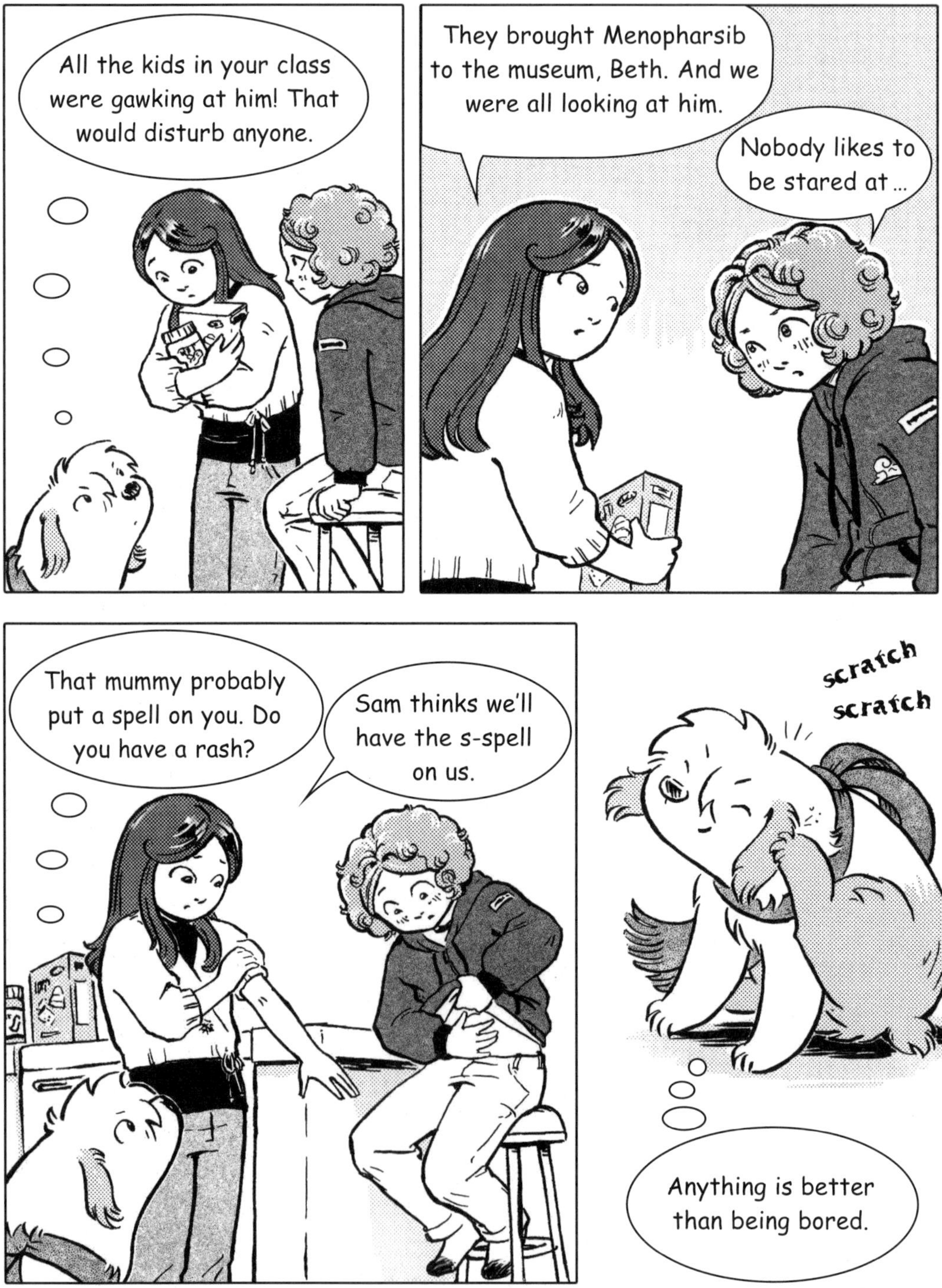
All the kids in your class were gawking at him! That would disturb anyone.
They brought Menopharsib to the museum, Beth. And we were all looking at him.
Nobody likes to be stared at ...
That mummy probably put a spell on you. Do you have a rash?
Sam thinks we'll have the s-spell on us.
scratch
scratch
Anything is better than being bored.

Later ...

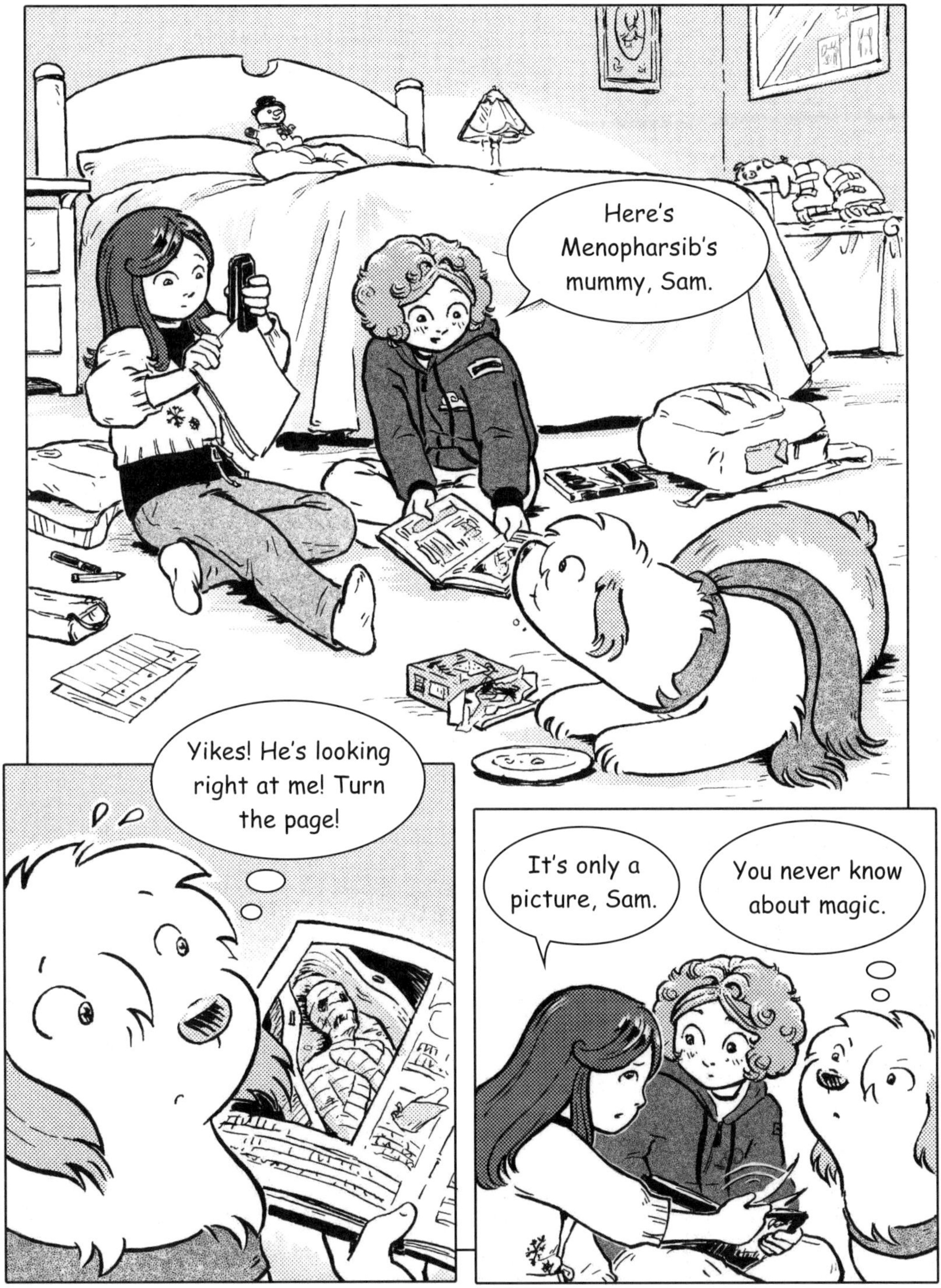
Here's Menopharsib's mummy, Sam.
Yikes! He's looking right at me! Turn the page!
It's only a picture, Sam.
You never know about magic.

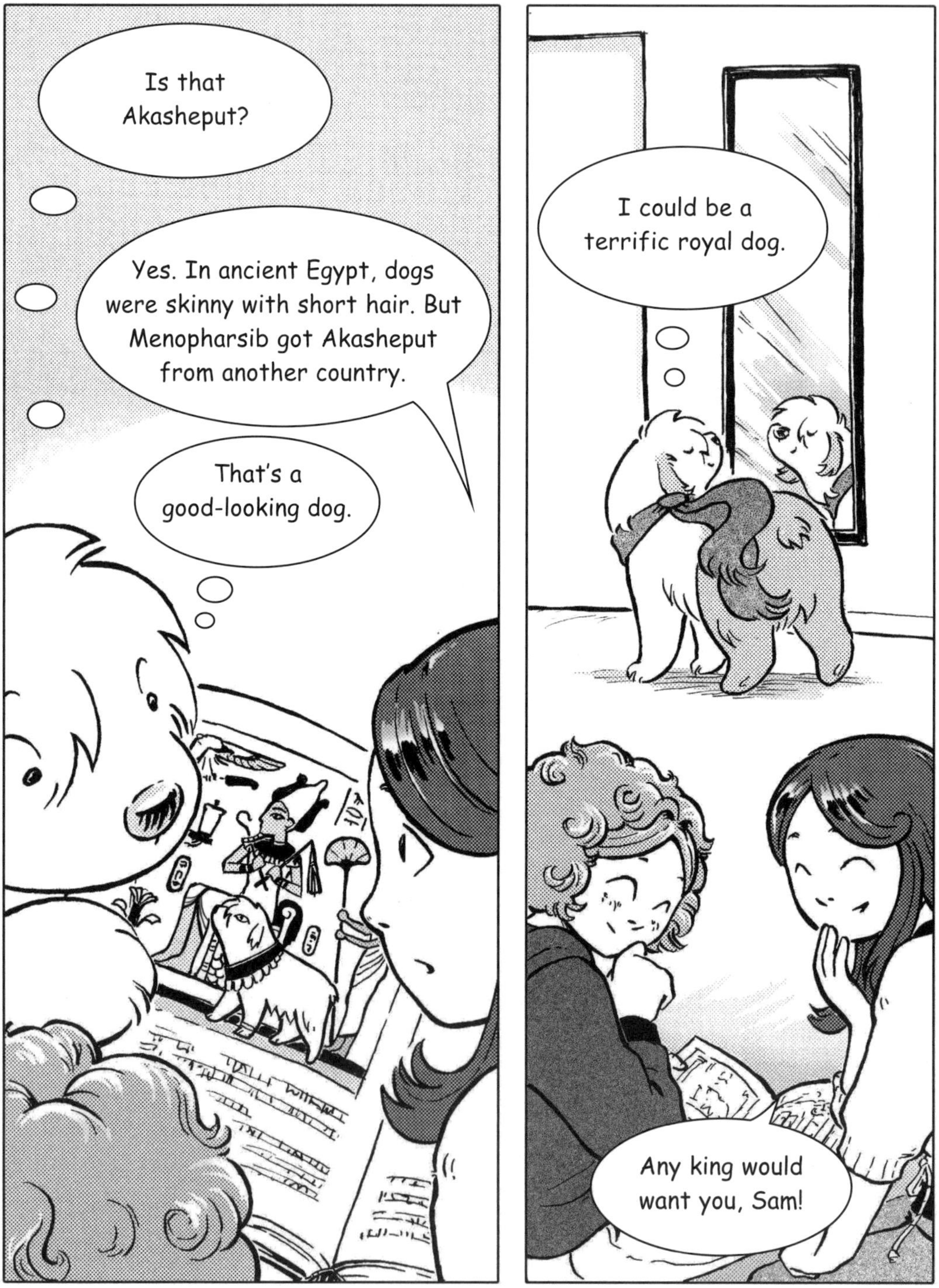
Is that Akasheput?
Yes. In ancient Egypt, dogs were skinny with short hair. But Menopharsib got Akasheput from another country.
That's a good-looking dog.
I could be a terrific royal dog.
Any king would want you, Sam!

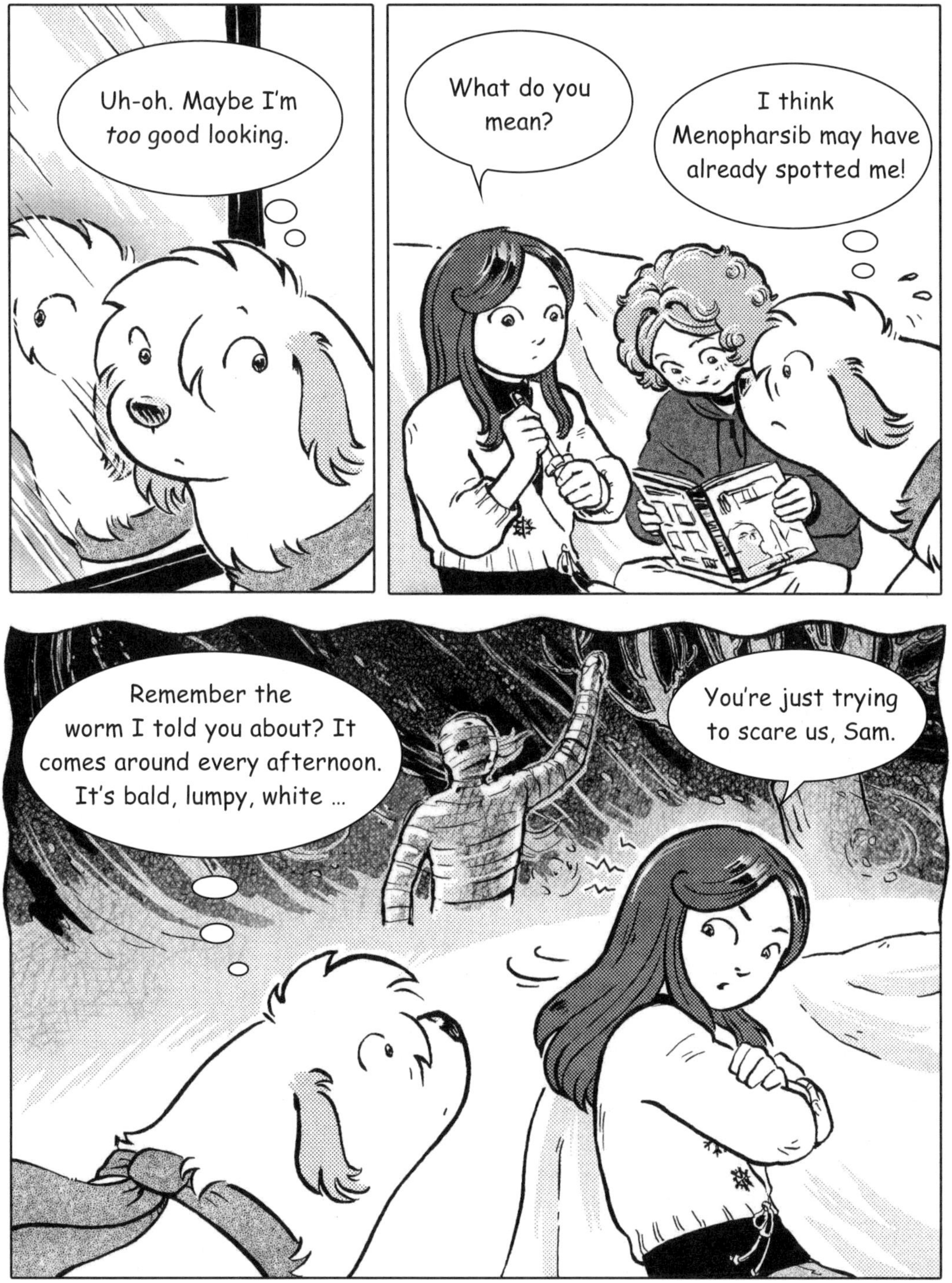
Uh-oh. Maybe I'm *too* good looking.
What do you mean?
I think Menopharsib may have already spotted me!
Remember the worm I told you about? It comes around every afternoon. It's bald, lumpy, white ...
You're just trying to scare us, Sam.

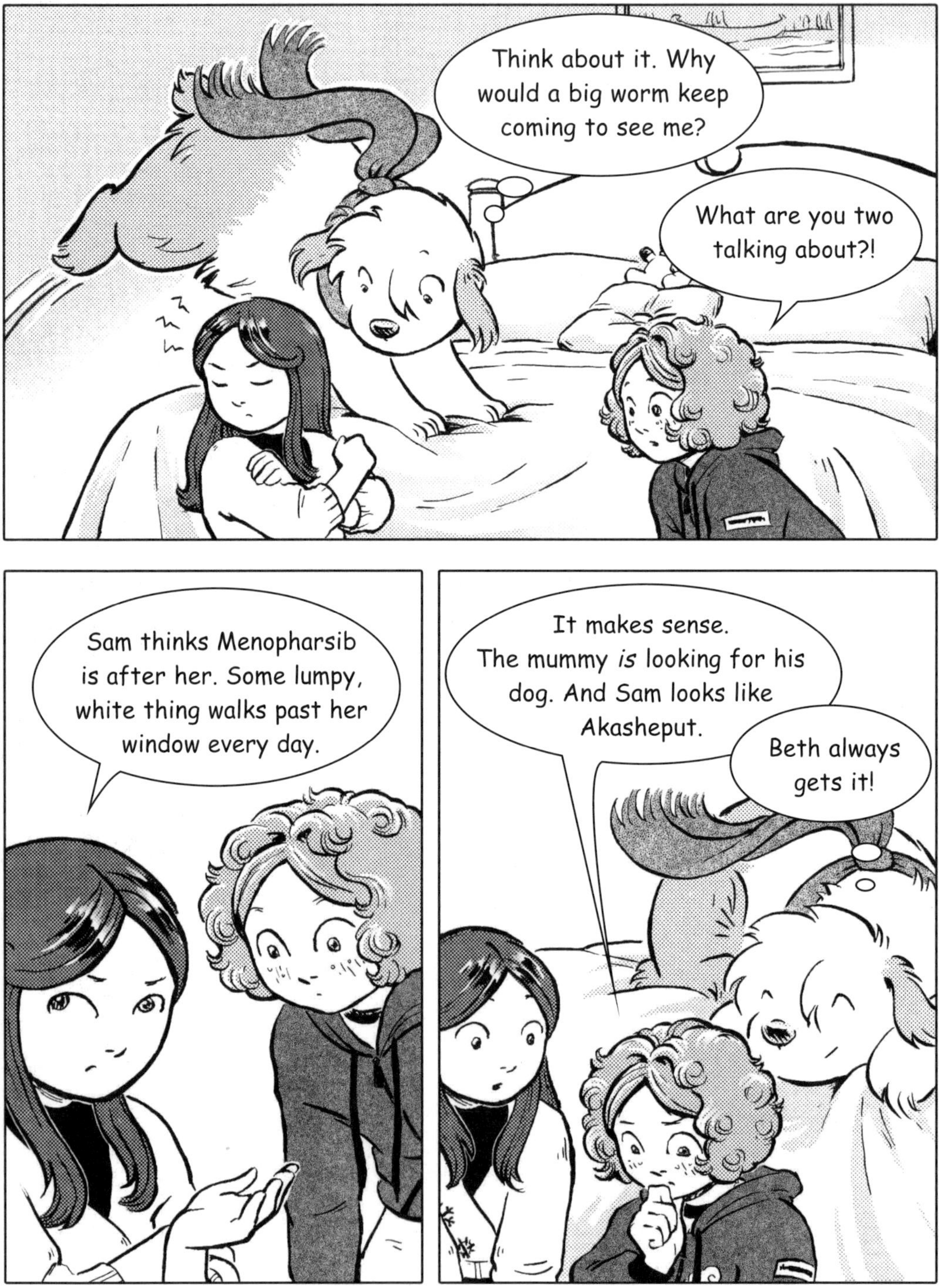
Think about it. Why would a big worm keep coming to see me?
What are you two talking about?!
Sam thinks Menopharsib is after her. Some lumpy, white thing walks past her window every day.
It makes sense. The mummy *is* looking for his dog. And Sam looks like Akasheput.
Beth always gets it!

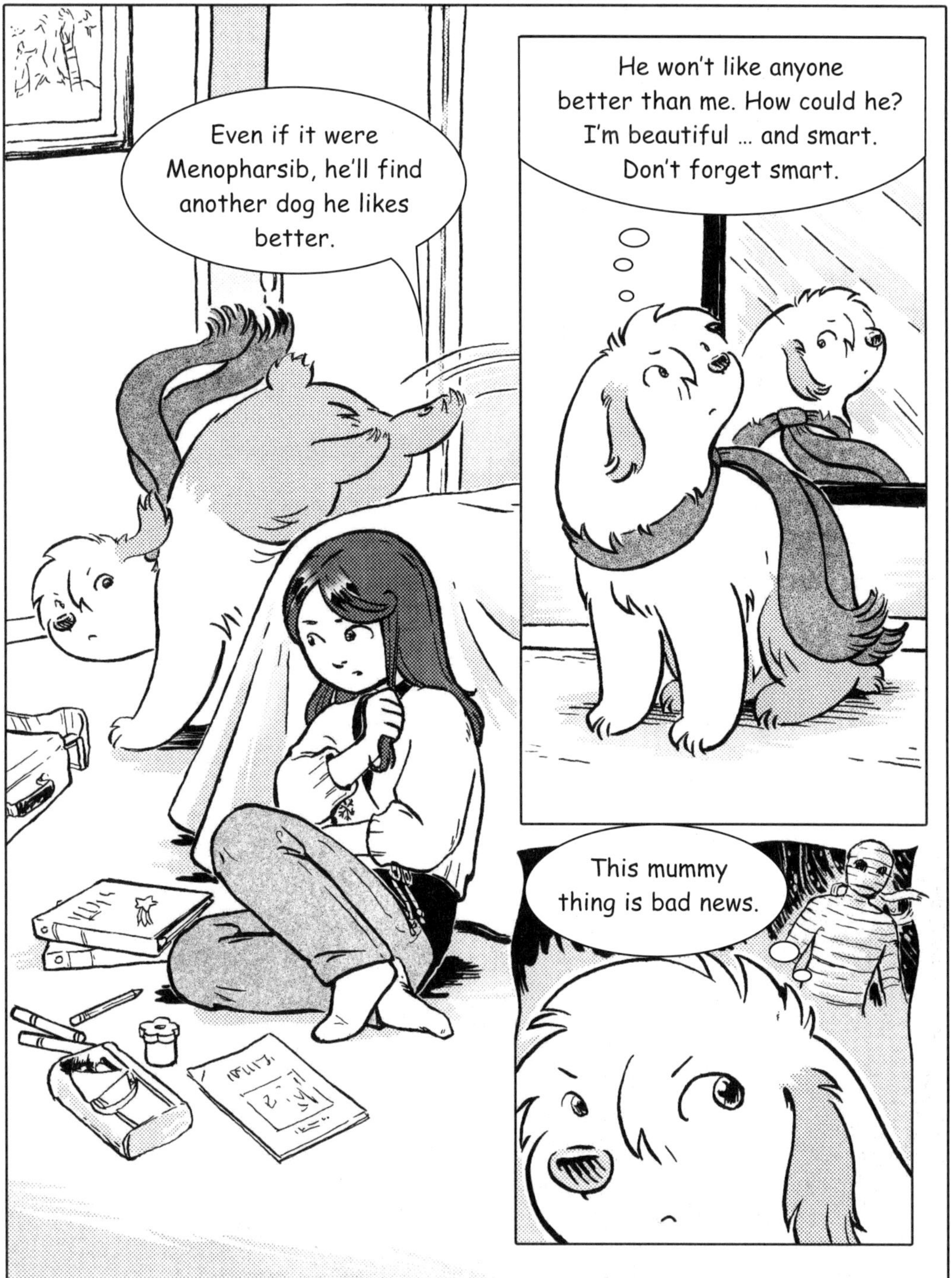
Even if it were Menopharsib, he'll find another dog he likes better.
He won't like anyone better than me. How could he? I'm beautiful ... and smart. Don't forget smart.
This mummy thing is bad news.

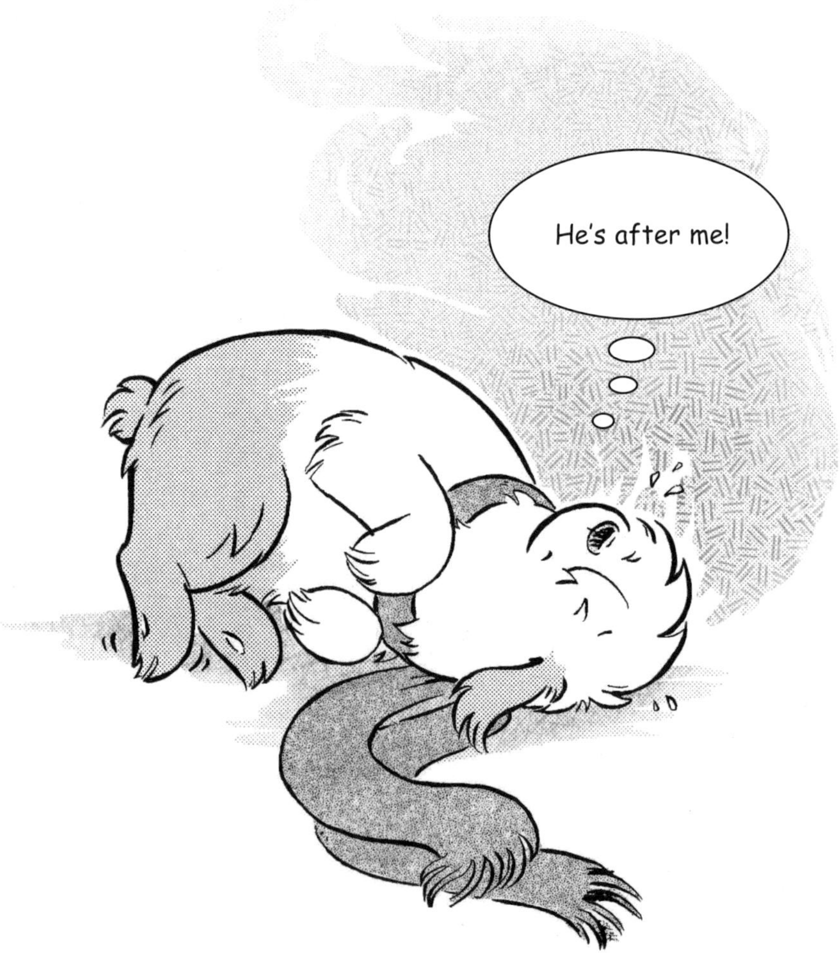
He's after me!

That night ...

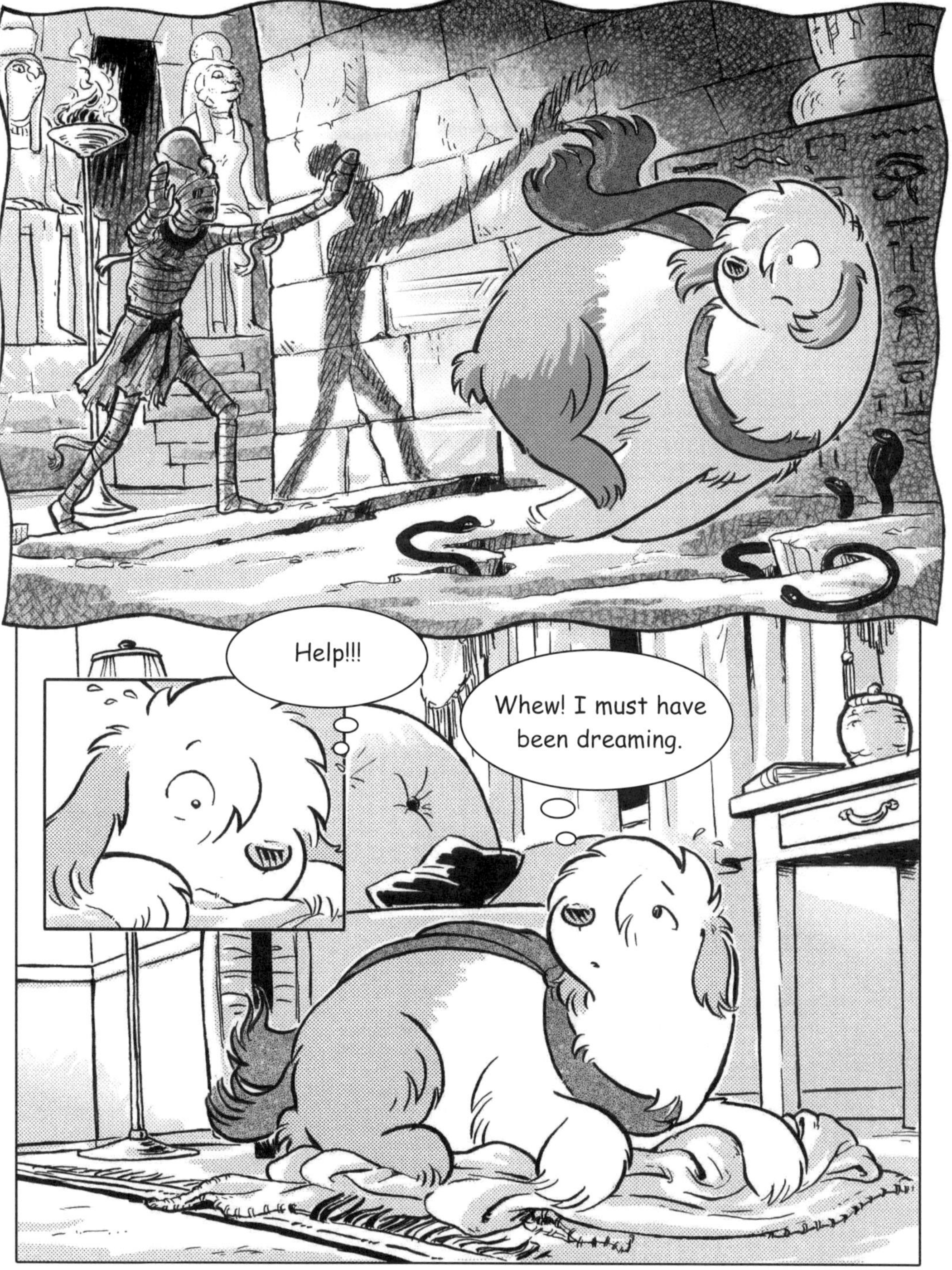
Help!!!
Whew! I must have been dreaming.

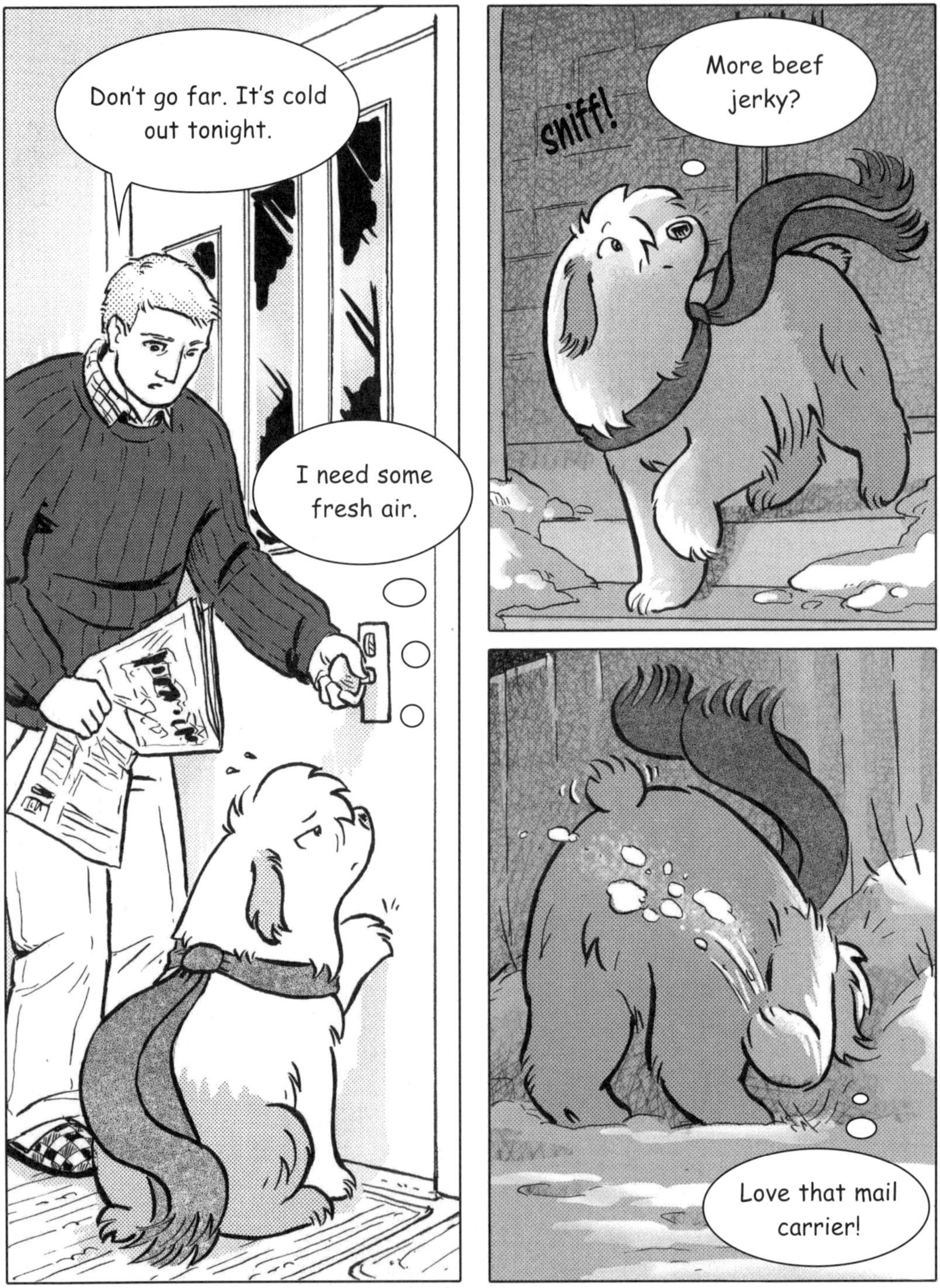
Don't go far. It's cold out tonight.
I need some fresh air.
sniff!
More beef jerky?
Love that mail carrier!

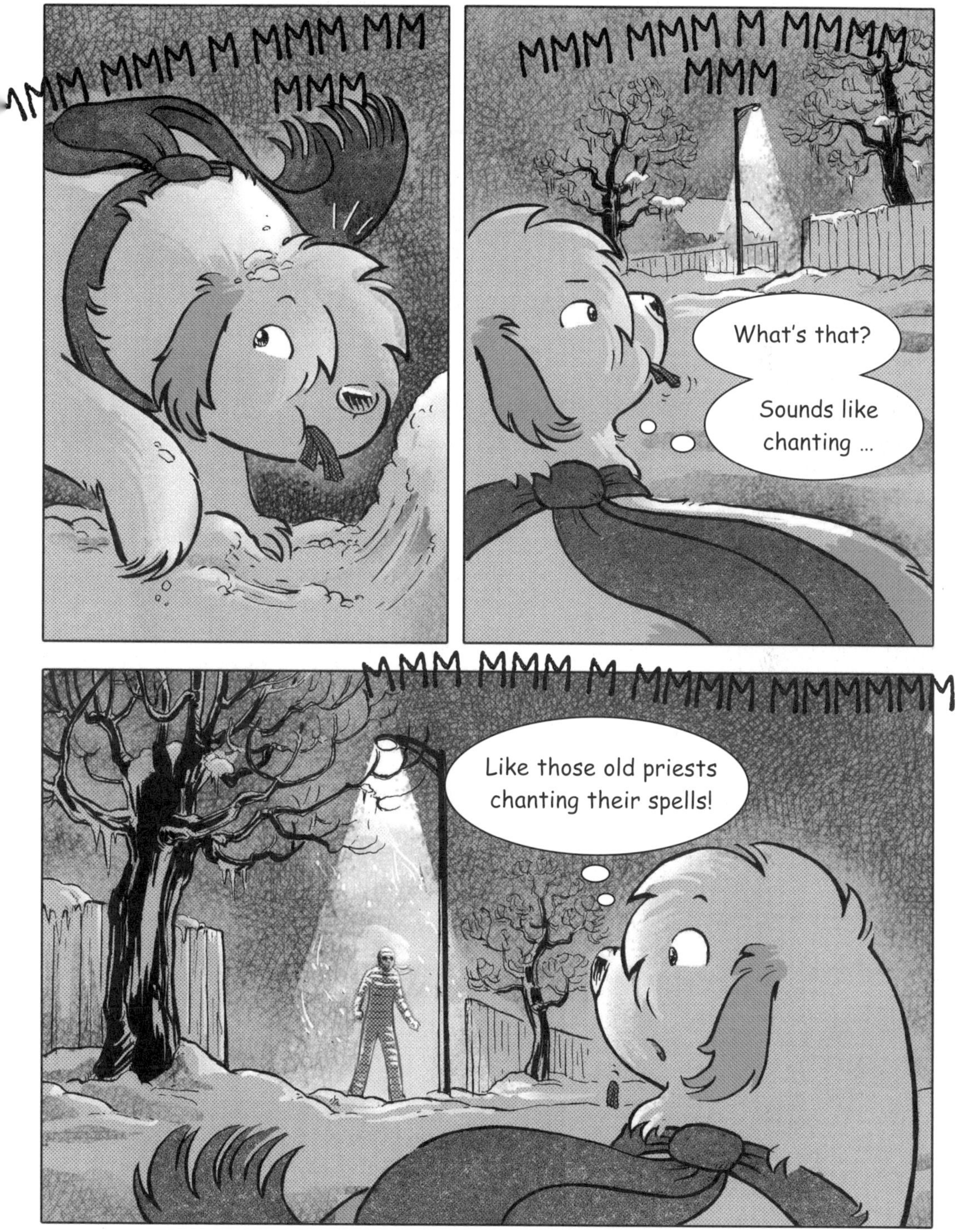
MMM MMM M MMM MM
MMM
MMM MMM M MMMM
MMM
What's that?
Sounds like chanting ...
MMM MMM M MMMM MMMMMM
Like those old priests chanting their spells!

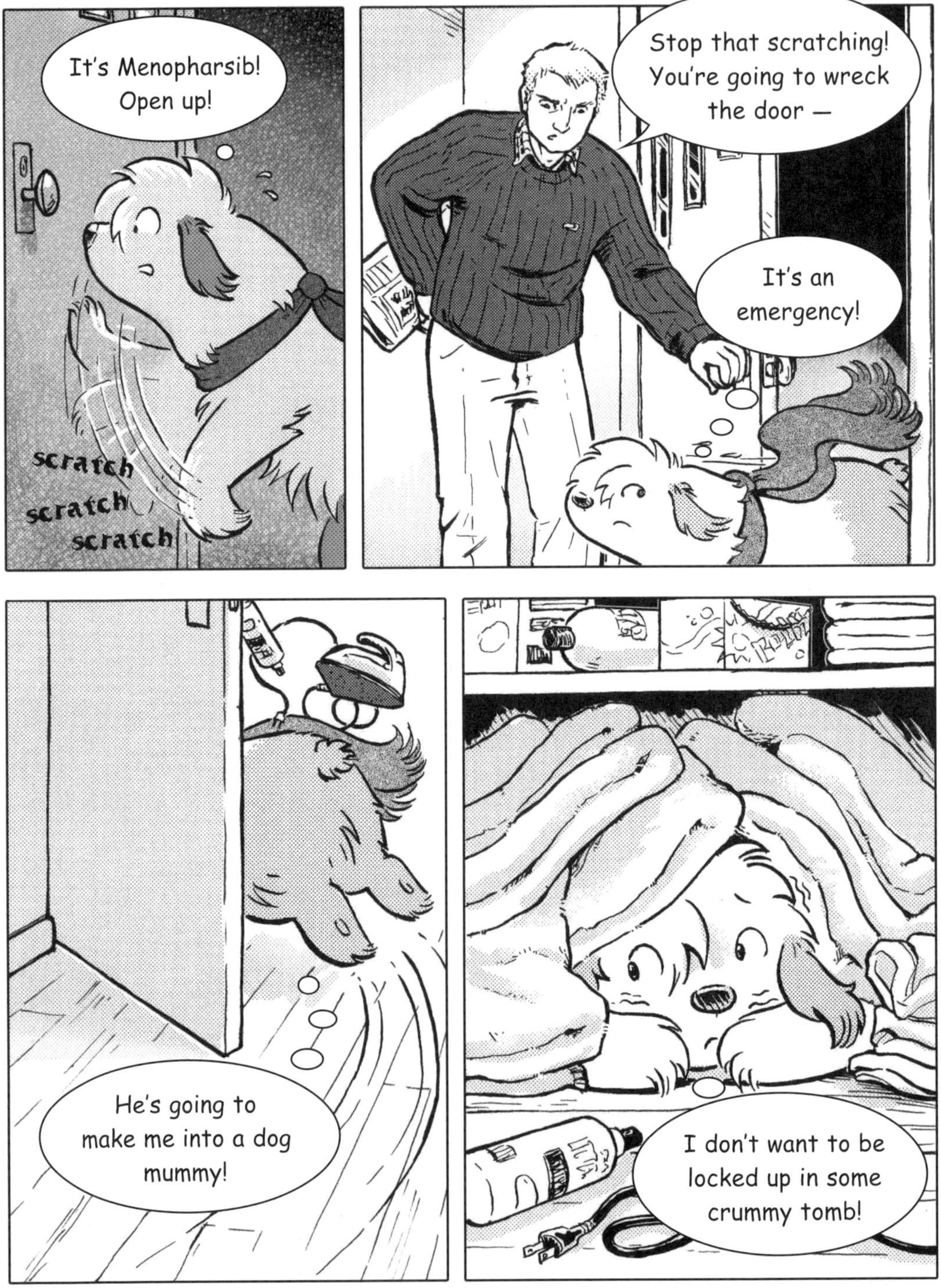
It's Menopharsib! Open up!
scratch
scratch
scratch
Stop that scratching! You're going to wreck the door —
It's an emergency!
He's going to make me into a dog mummy!
I don't want to be locked up in some crummy tomb!

The next afternoon ...

Soon ...

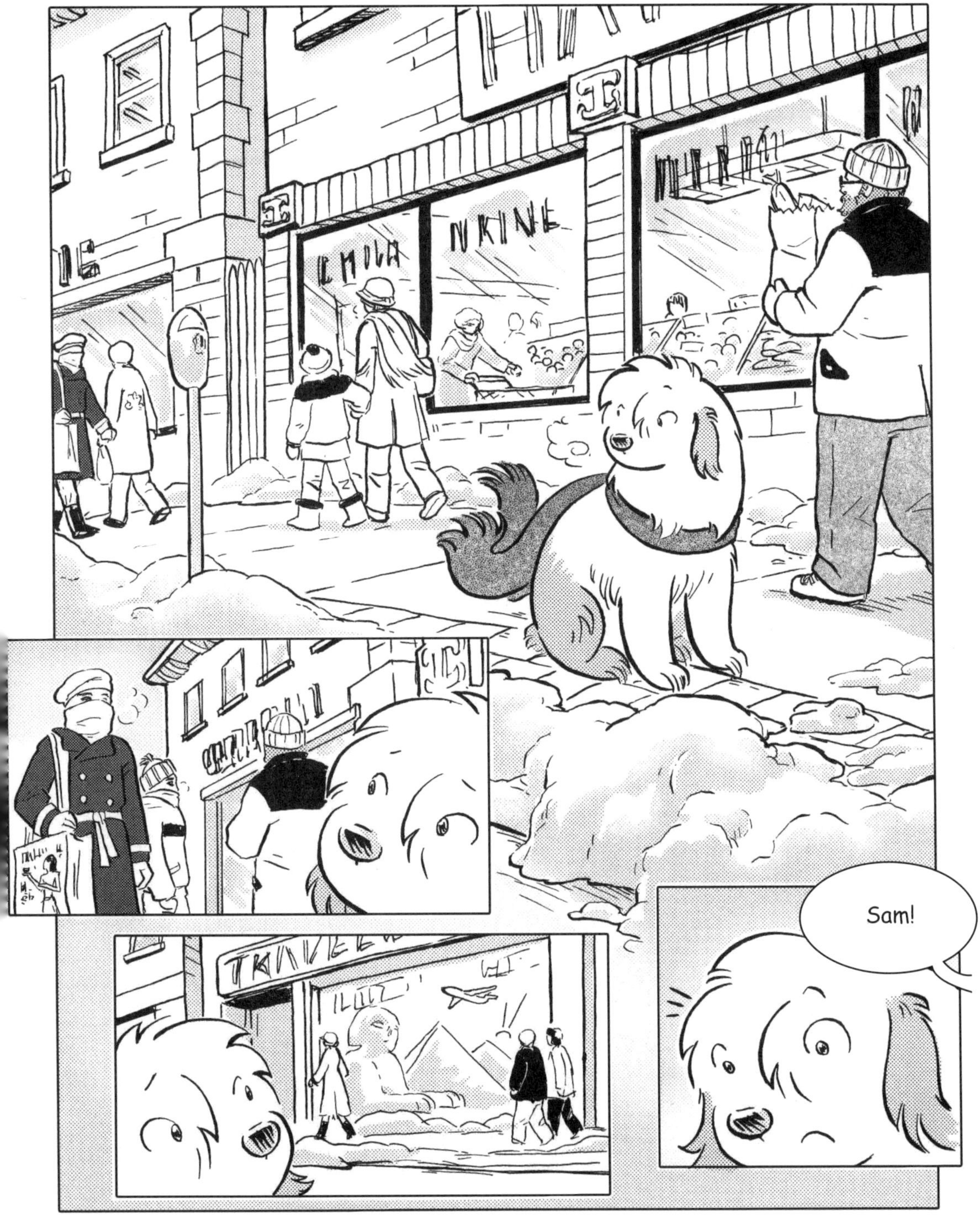

Sam!

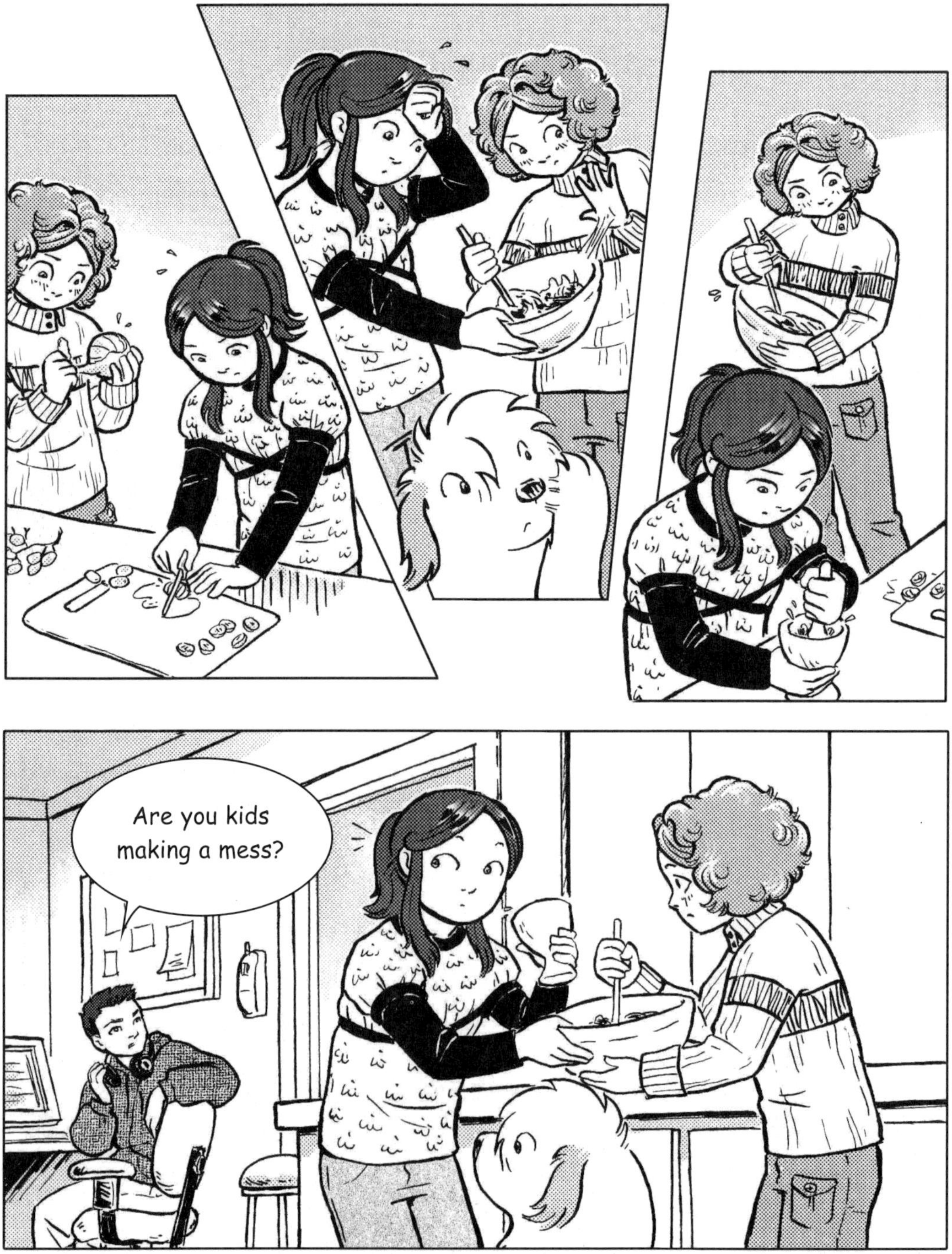
Are you kids making a mess?

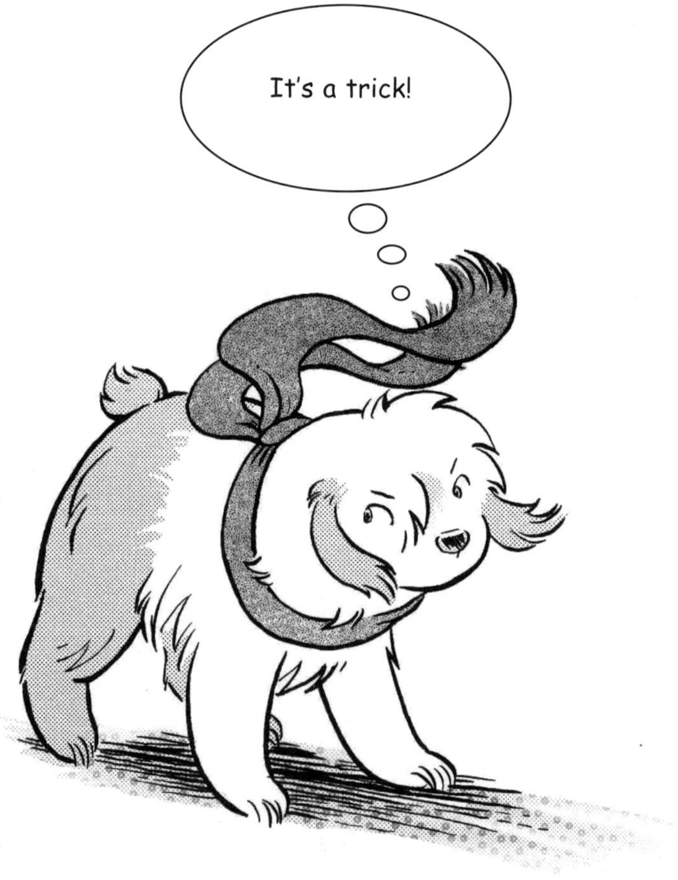
It's a trick!

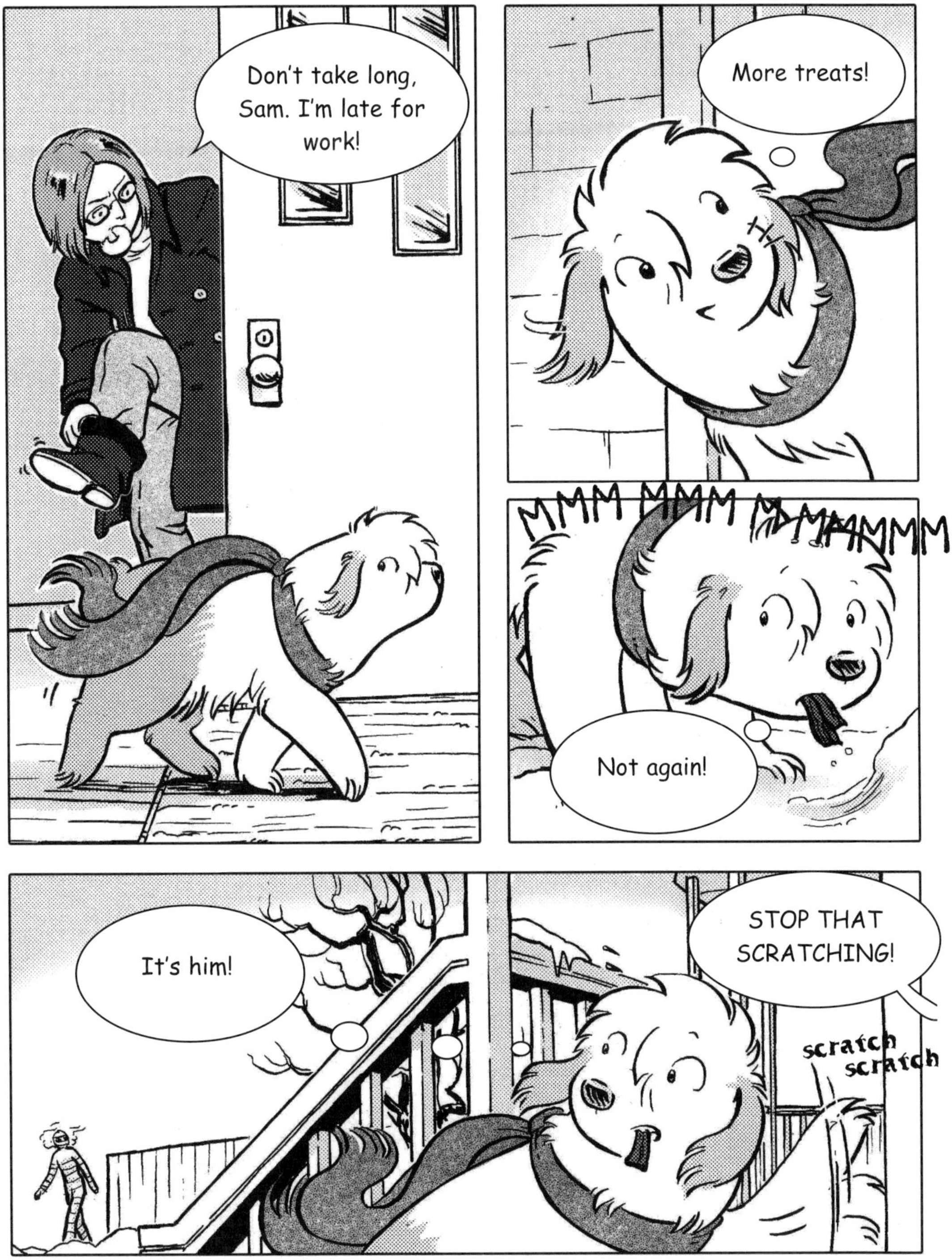
Don't take long, Sam. I'm late for work!
More treats!
MMM MMM MMMMMM
Not again!
It's him!
STOP THAT SCRATCHING!
scratch scratch

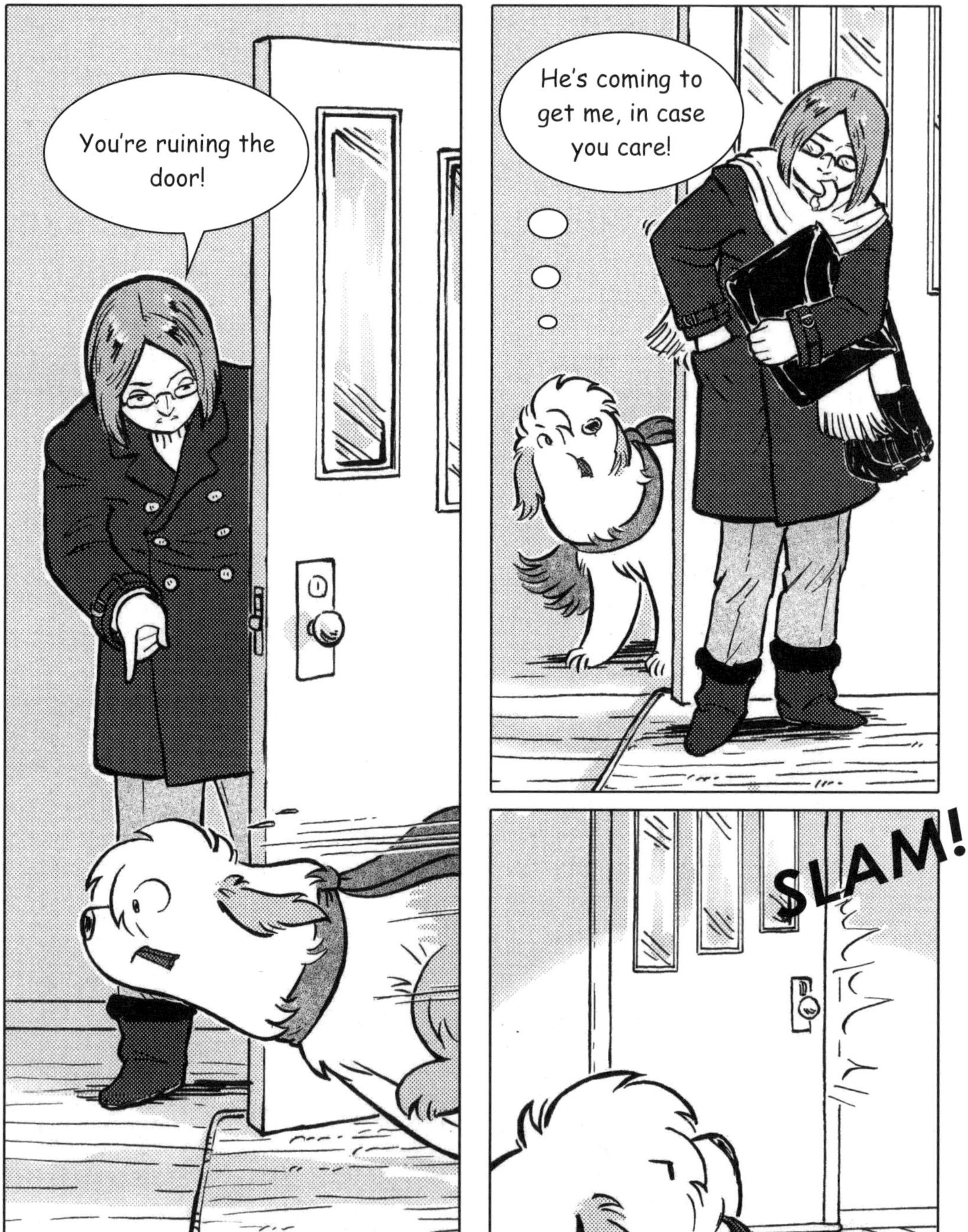
You're ruining the door!
He's coming to get me, in case you care!
SLAM!

57

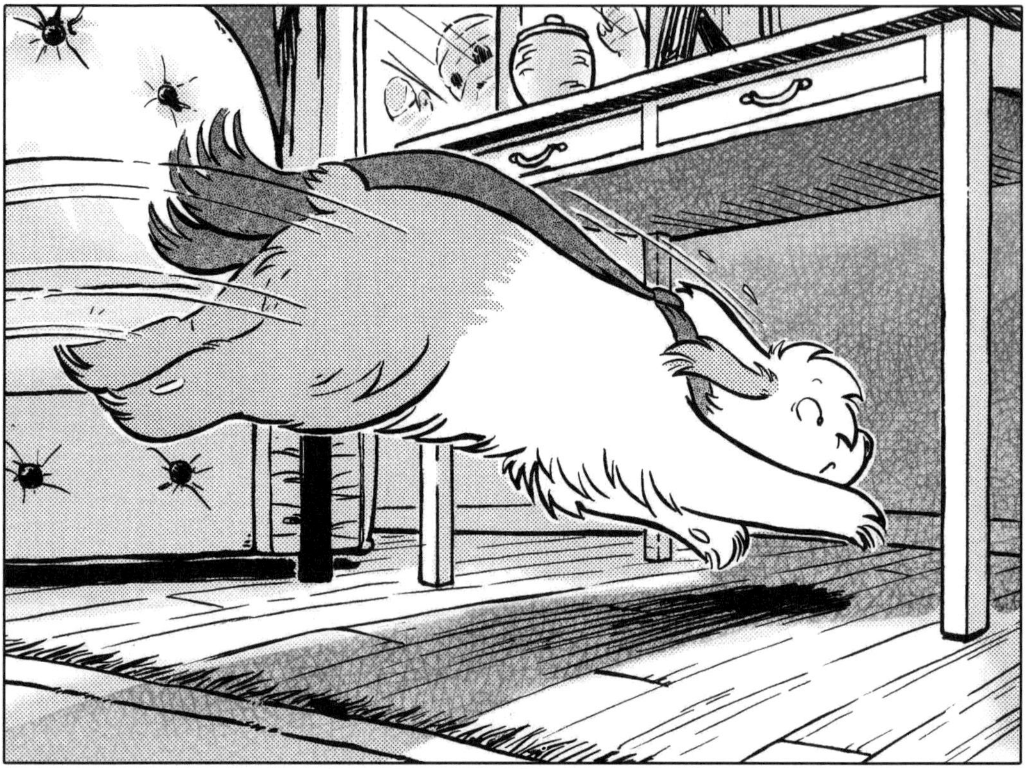

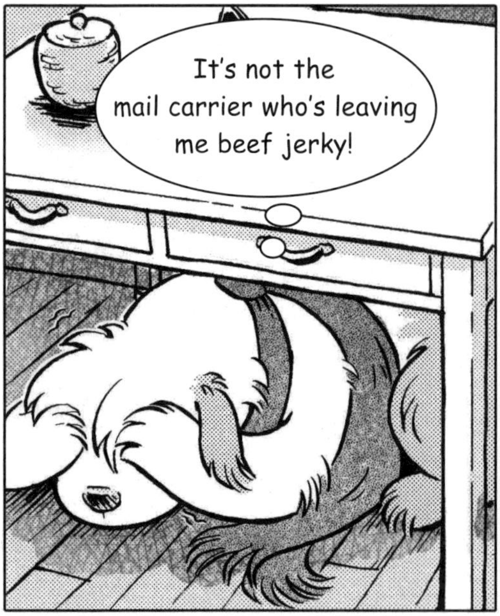
It's not the mail carrier who's leaving me beef jerky!

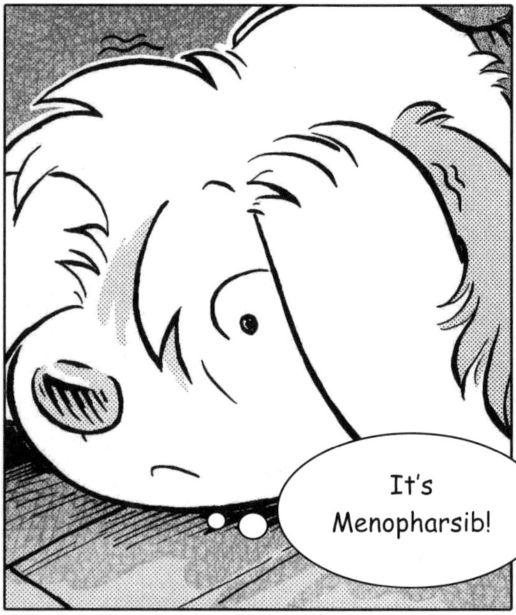
It's Menopharsib!

That afternoon ...

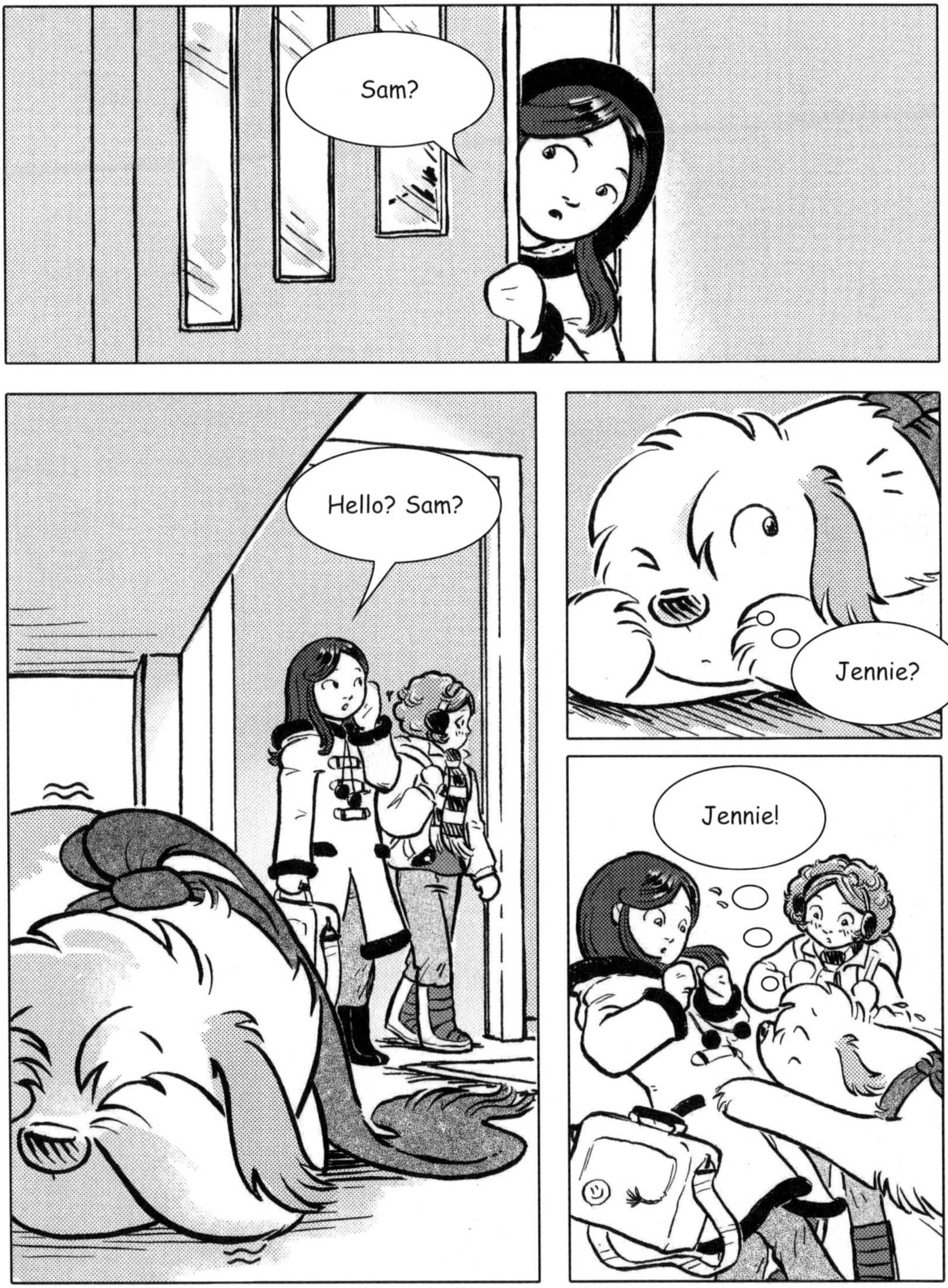

Sam?
Hello? Sam?
Jennie?
Jennie!

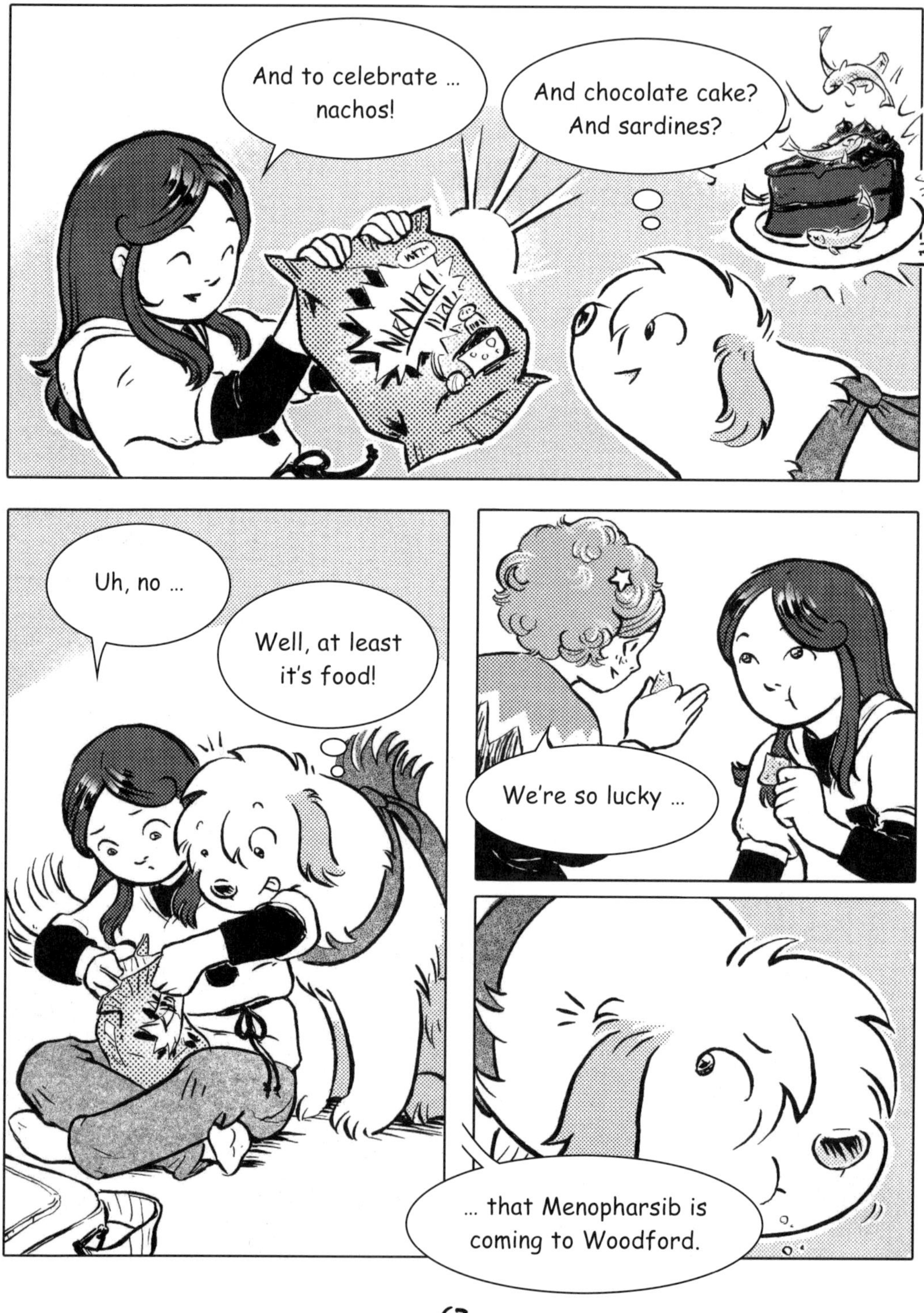
And to celebrate ... nachos!
And chocolate cake? And sardines?
Uh, no ...
Well, at least it's food!
We're so lucky ...
... that Menopharsib is coming to Woodford.

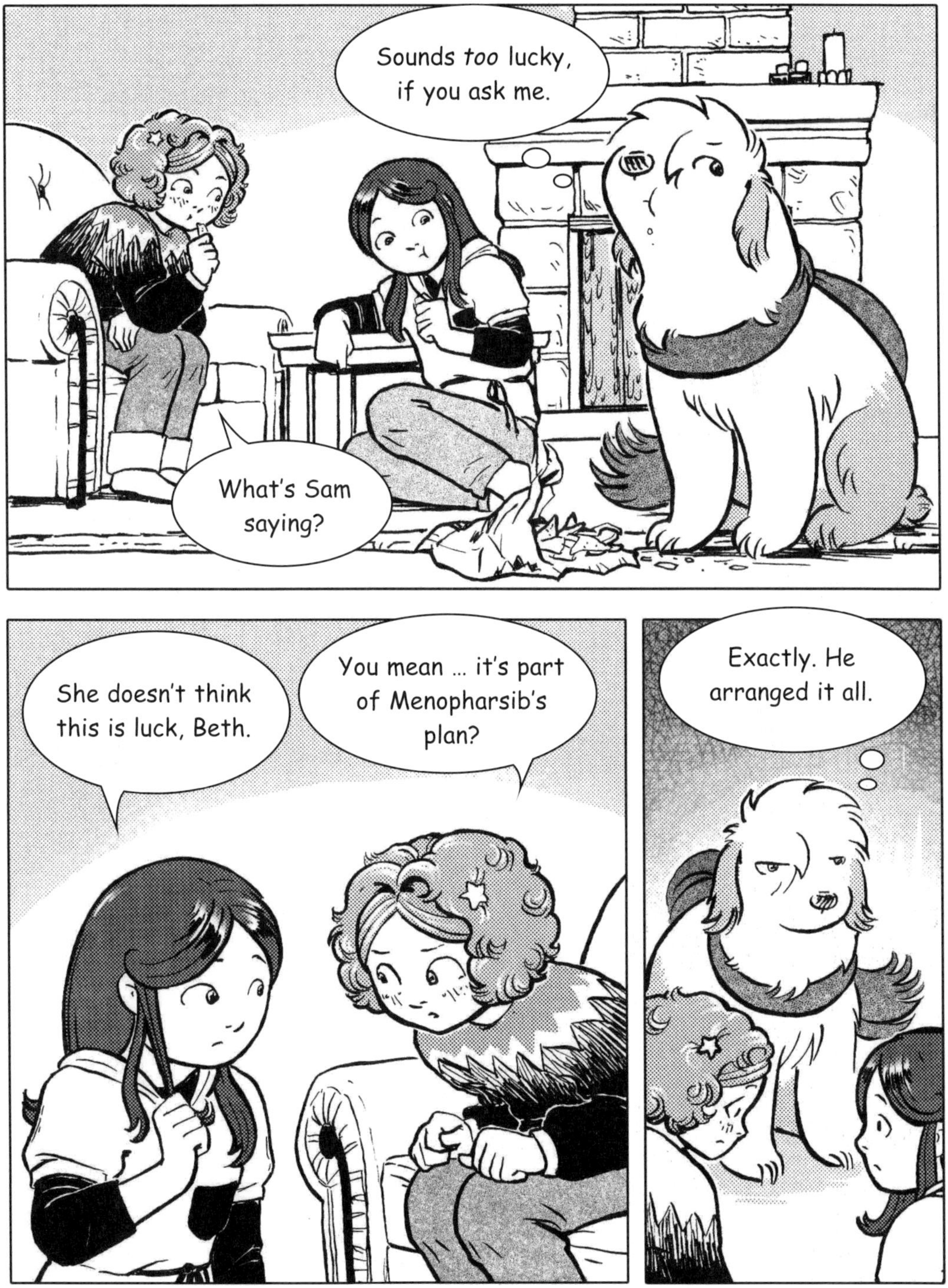
Sounds *too* lucky, if you ask me.
What's Sam saying?
She doesn't think this is luck, Beth.
You mean ... it's part of Menopharsib's plan?
Exactly. He arranged it all.

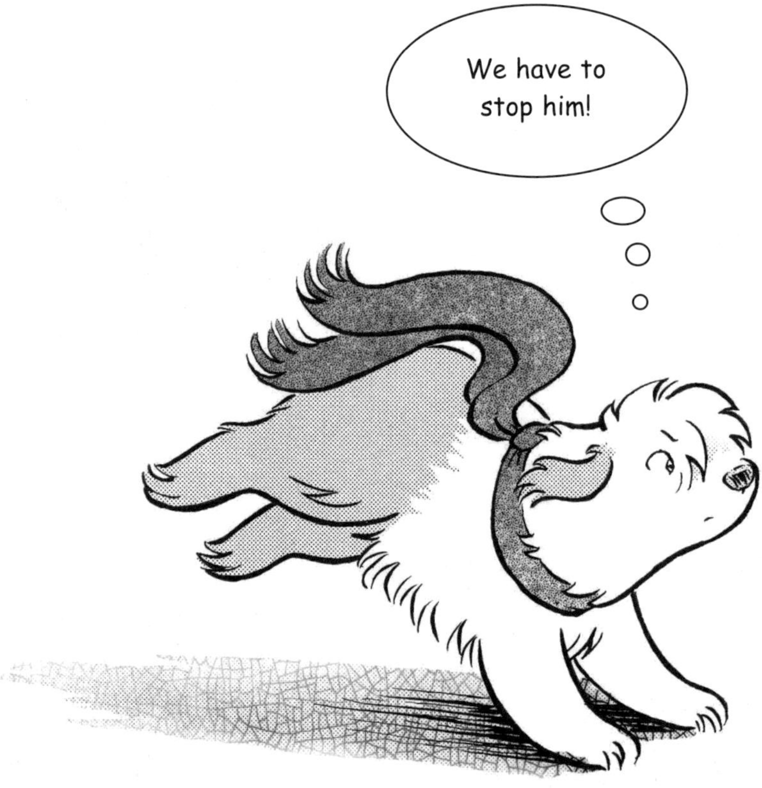
We have to stop him!

The next morning ...

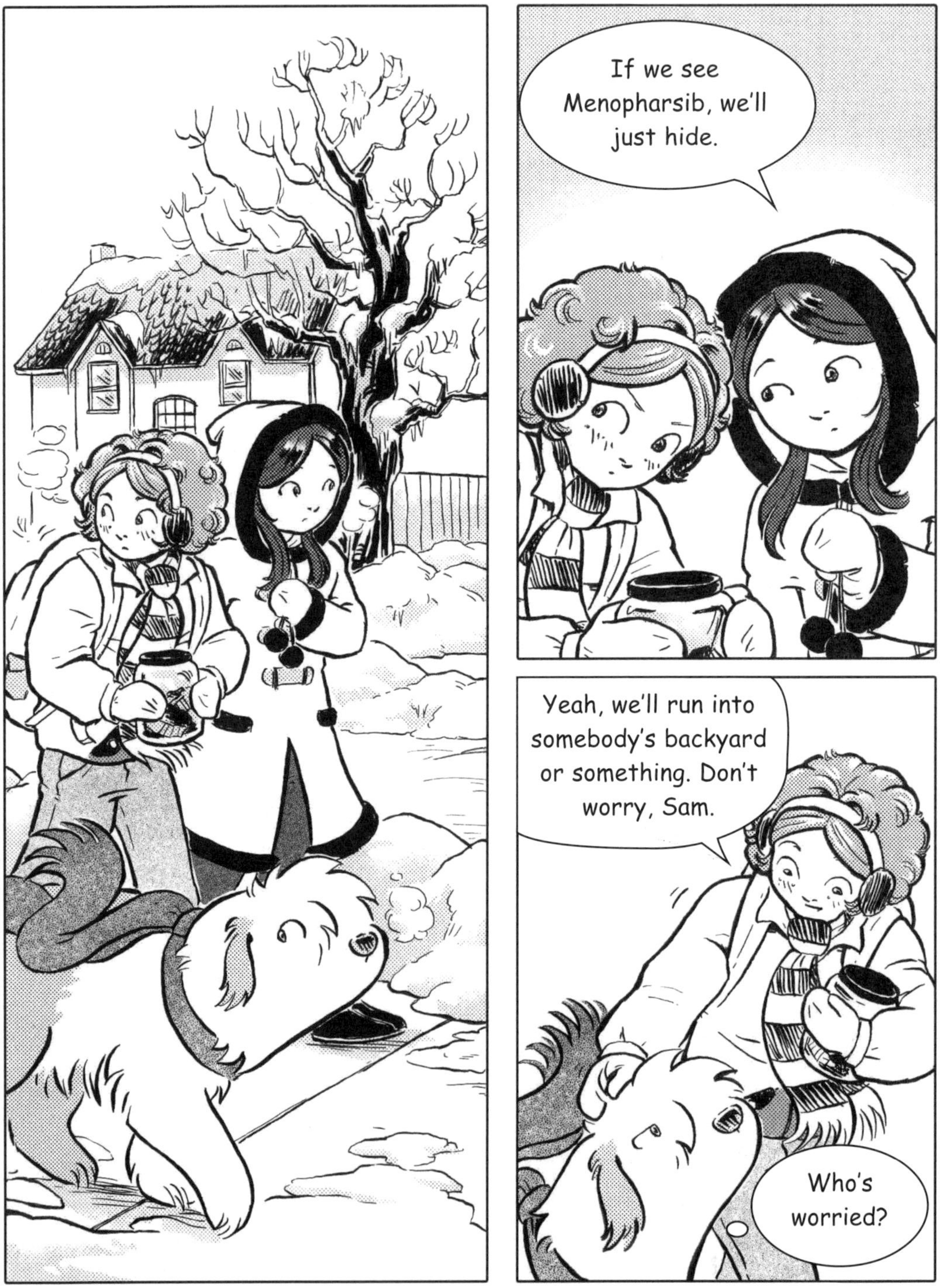
If we see Menopharsib, we'll just hide.
Yeah, we'll run into somebody's backyard or something. Don't worry, Sam.
Who's worried?

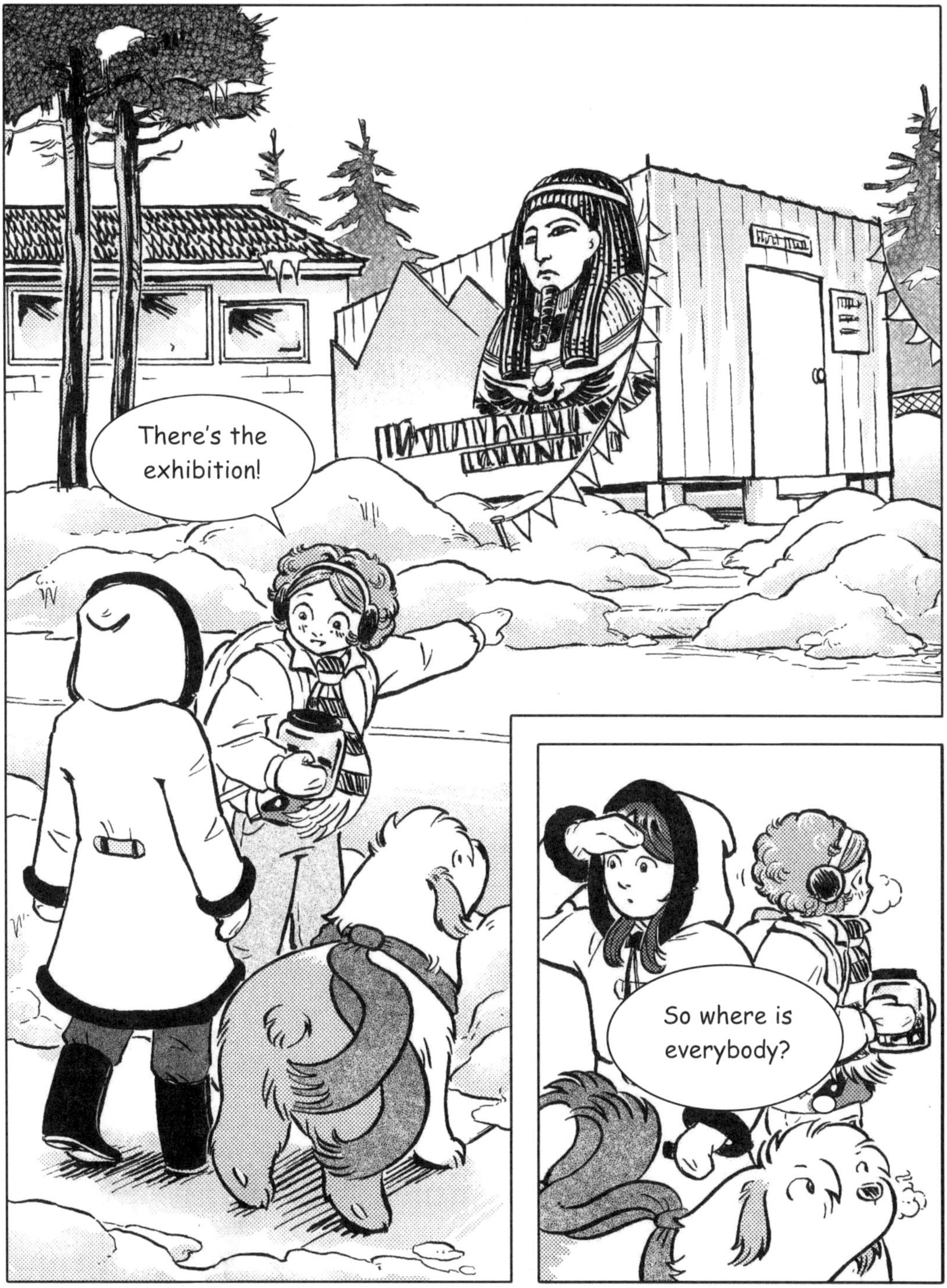
There's the exhibition!
So where is everybody?

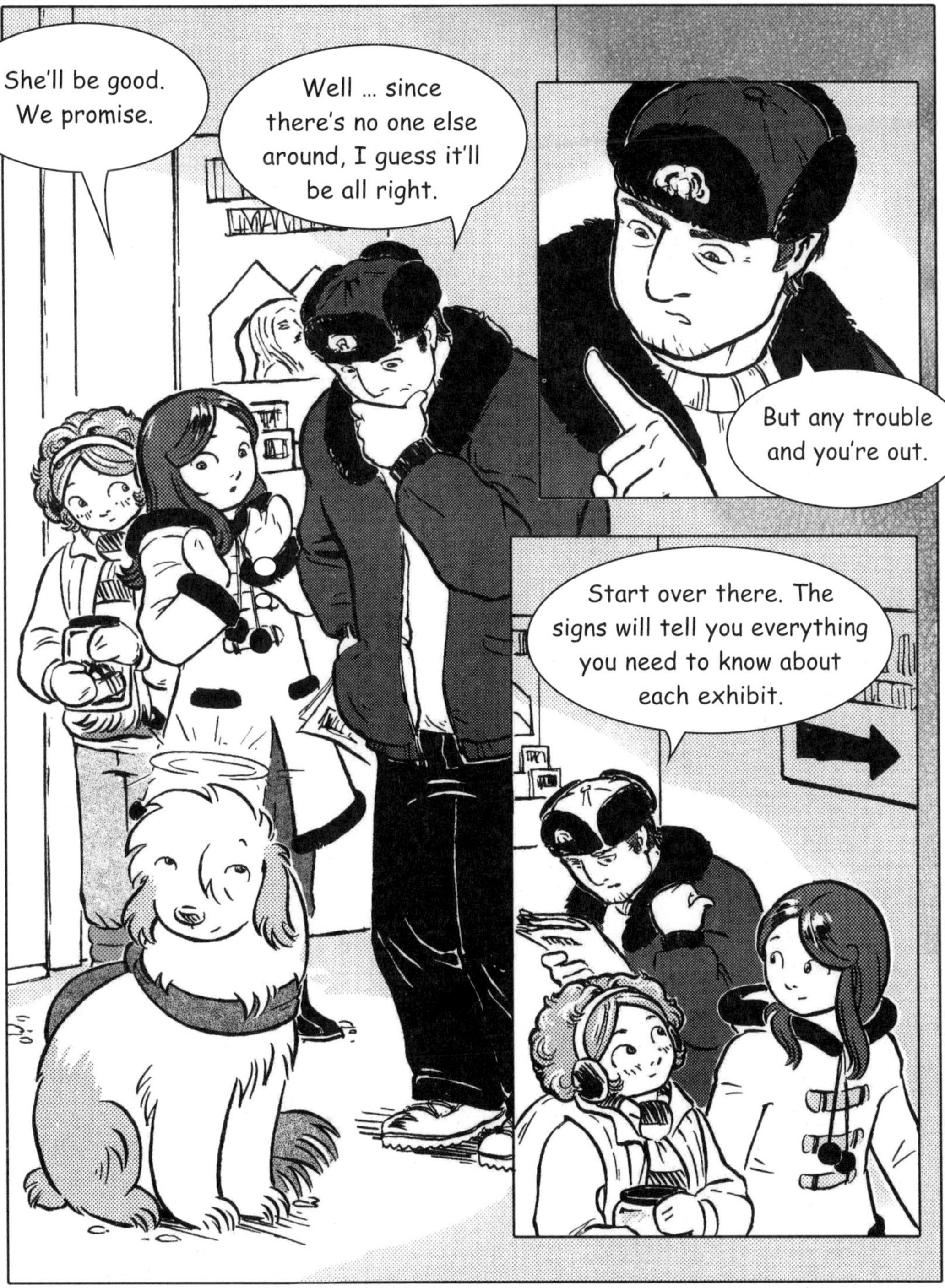
She'll be good. We promise.
Well ... since there's no one else around, I guess it'll be all right.
But any trouble and you're out.
Start over there. The signs will tell you everything you need to know about each exhibit.

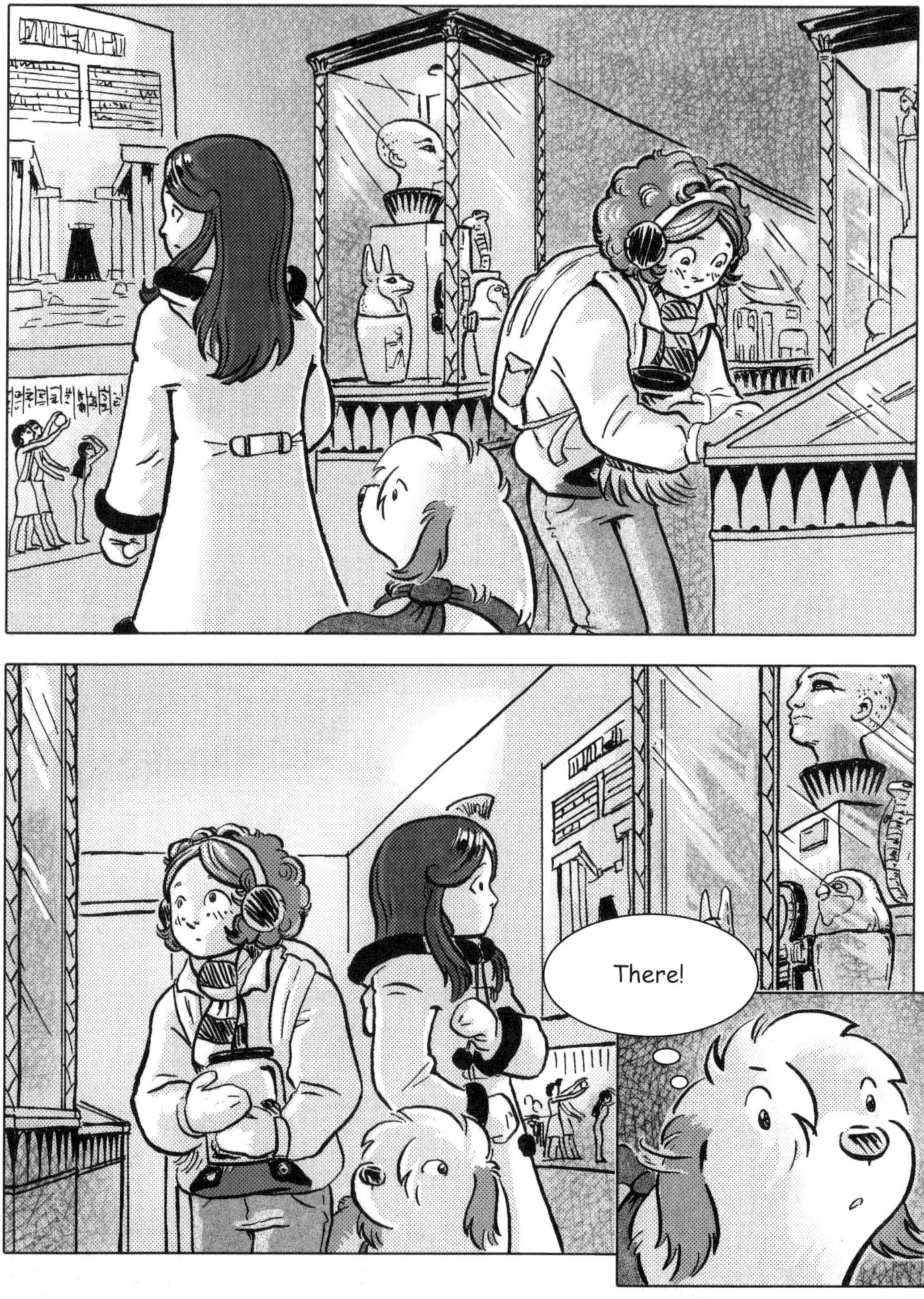
There!

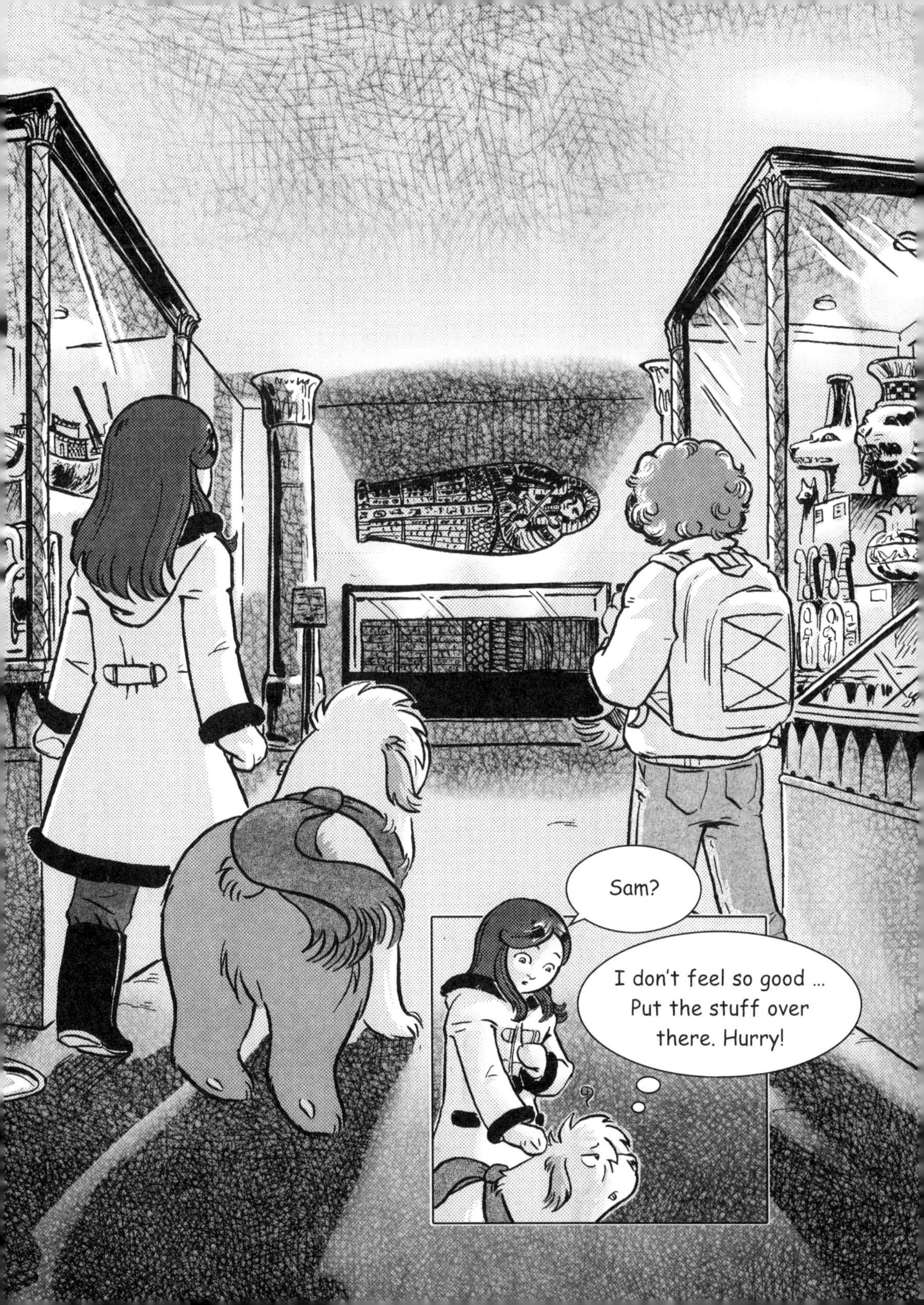
Sam?
I don't feel so good ... Put the stuff over there. Hurry!

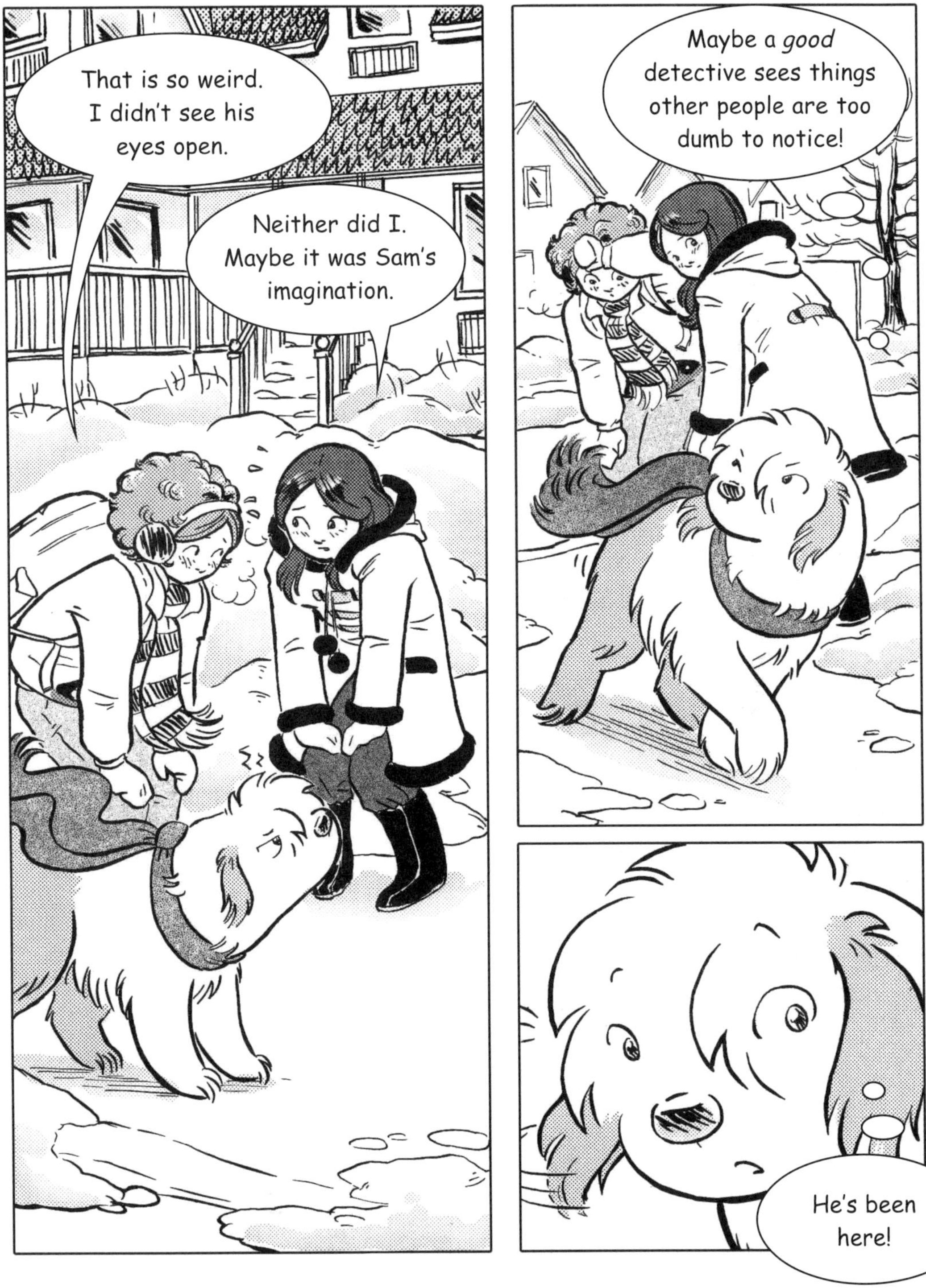
That is so weird. I didn't see his eyes open.
Neither did I. Maybe it was Sam's imagination.
Maybe a *good* detective sees things other people are too dumb to notice!
He's been here!

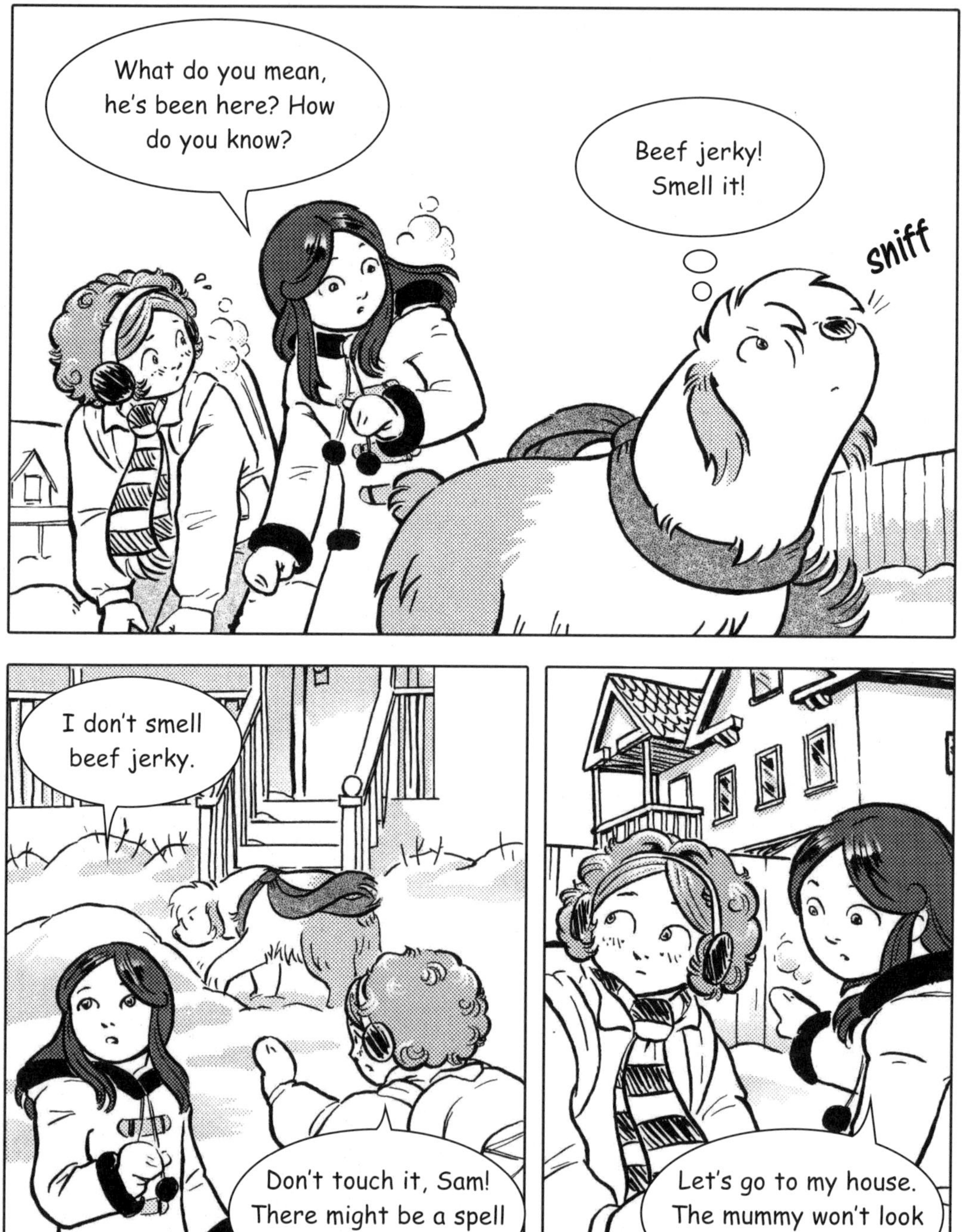
What do you mean, he's been here? How do you know?
Beef jerky! Smell it!
SNIFF
I don't smell beef jerky.
Don't touch it, Sam! There might be a spell on it. Or poison!
Let's go to my house. The mummy won't look for Sam there.

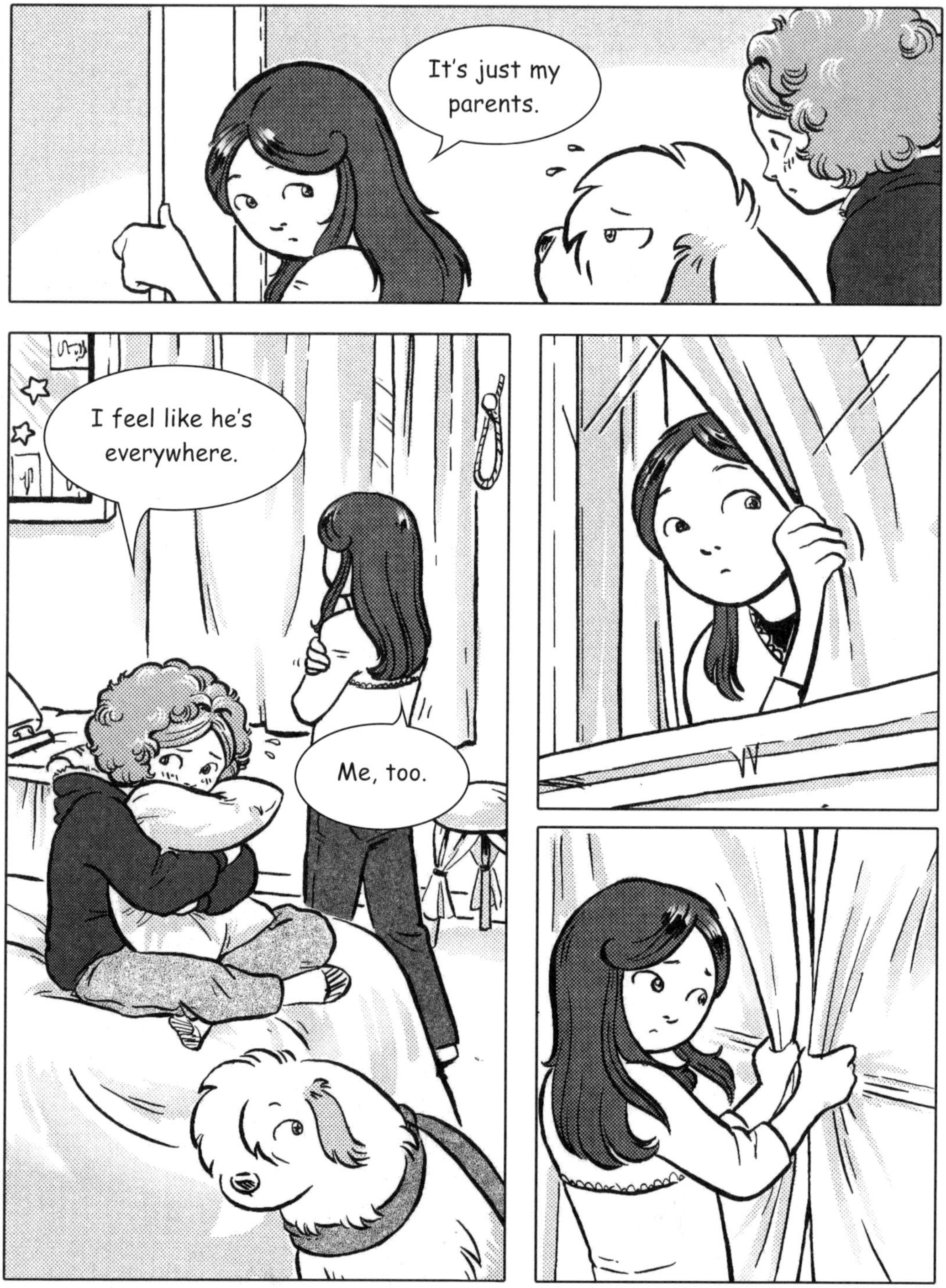
It's just my parents.
I feel like he's everywhere.
Me, too.

Hours later ...

85

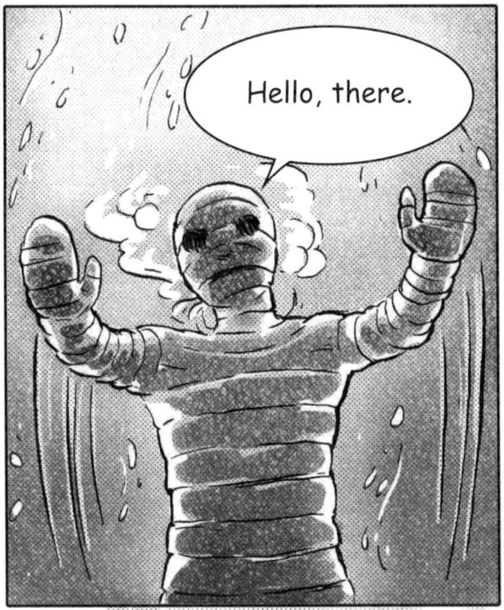
Hello, there.

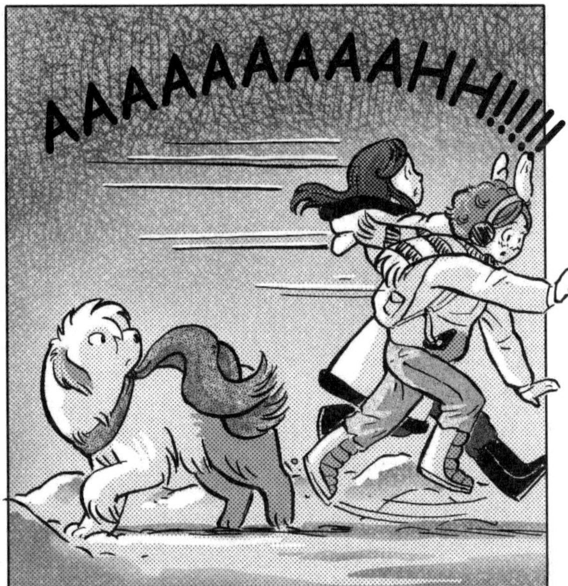
AAAAAAAAAAHH!!!!!!

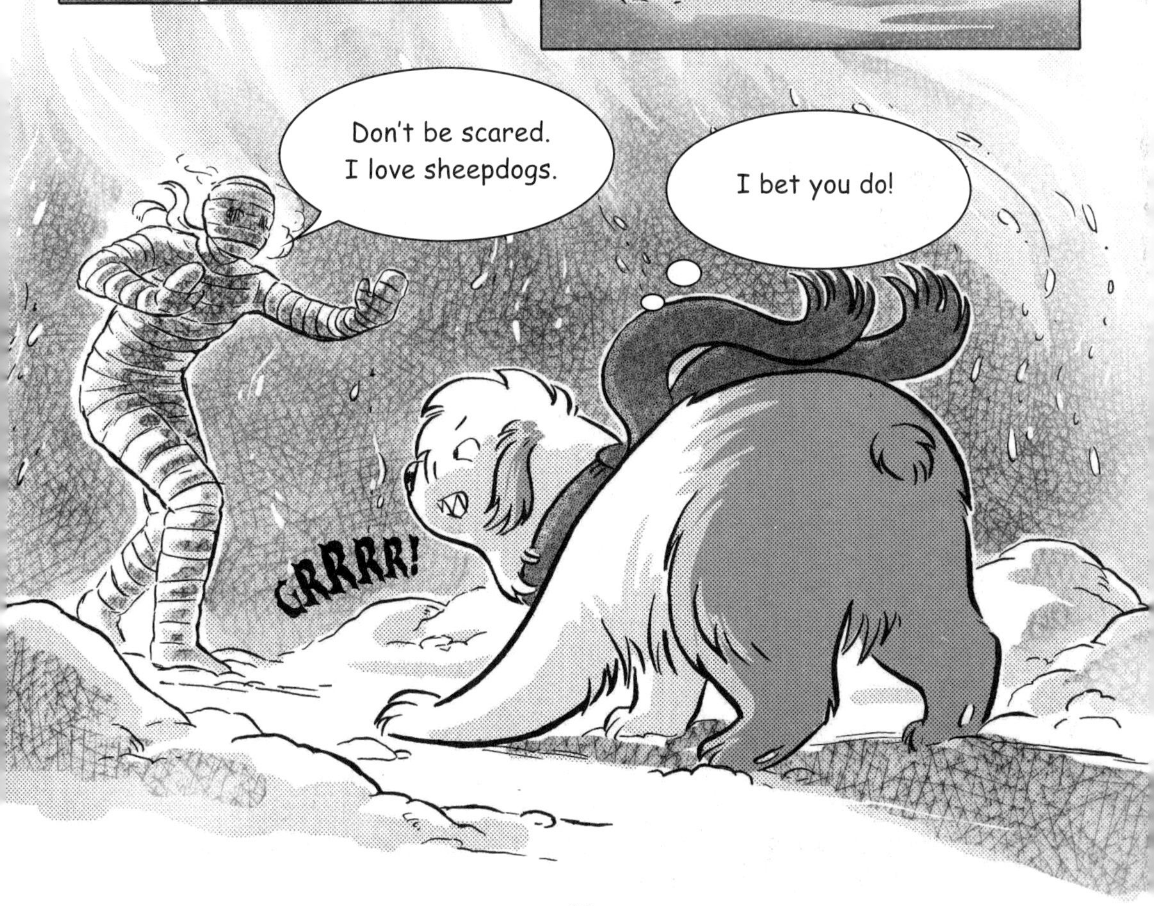
Don't be scared.
I love sheepdogs.
I bet you do!
GRRRR!

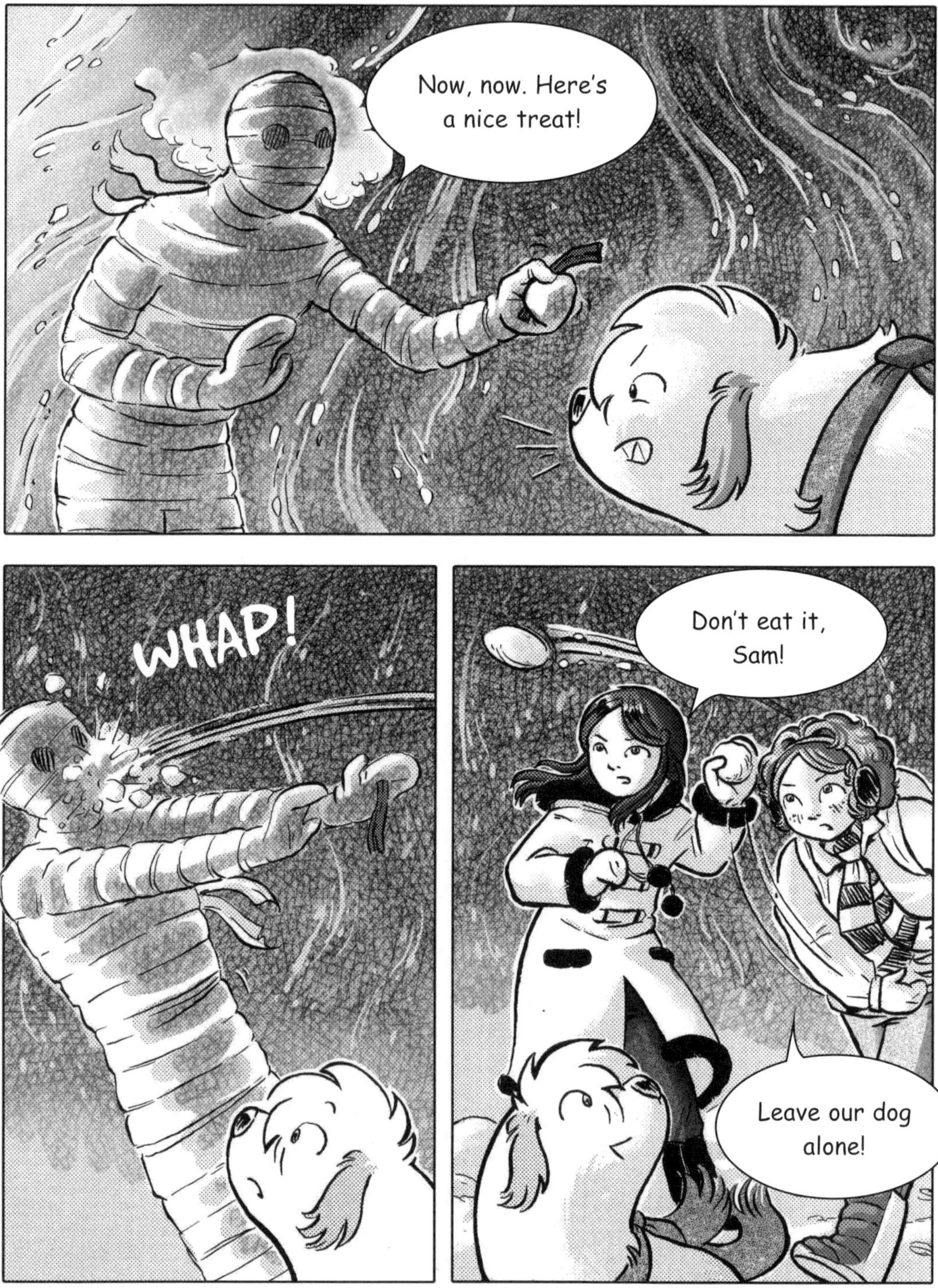
Now, now. Here's a nice treat!
WHAP!
Don't eat it, Sam!
Leave our dog alone!

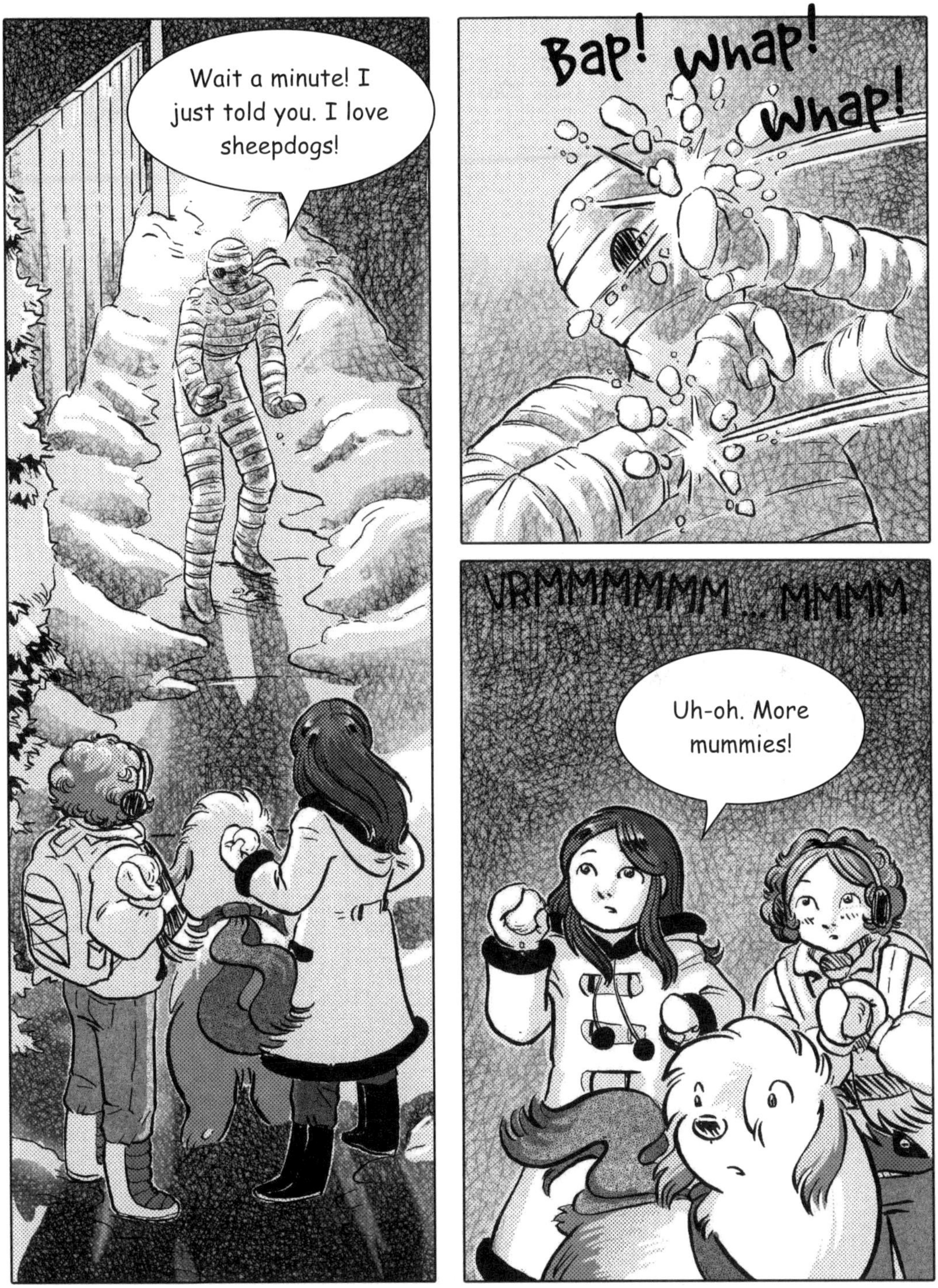
Wait a minute! I just told you. I love sheepdogs!
Bap! whap! whap!
VRMMMMMM ... MMMM
Uh-oh. More mummies!

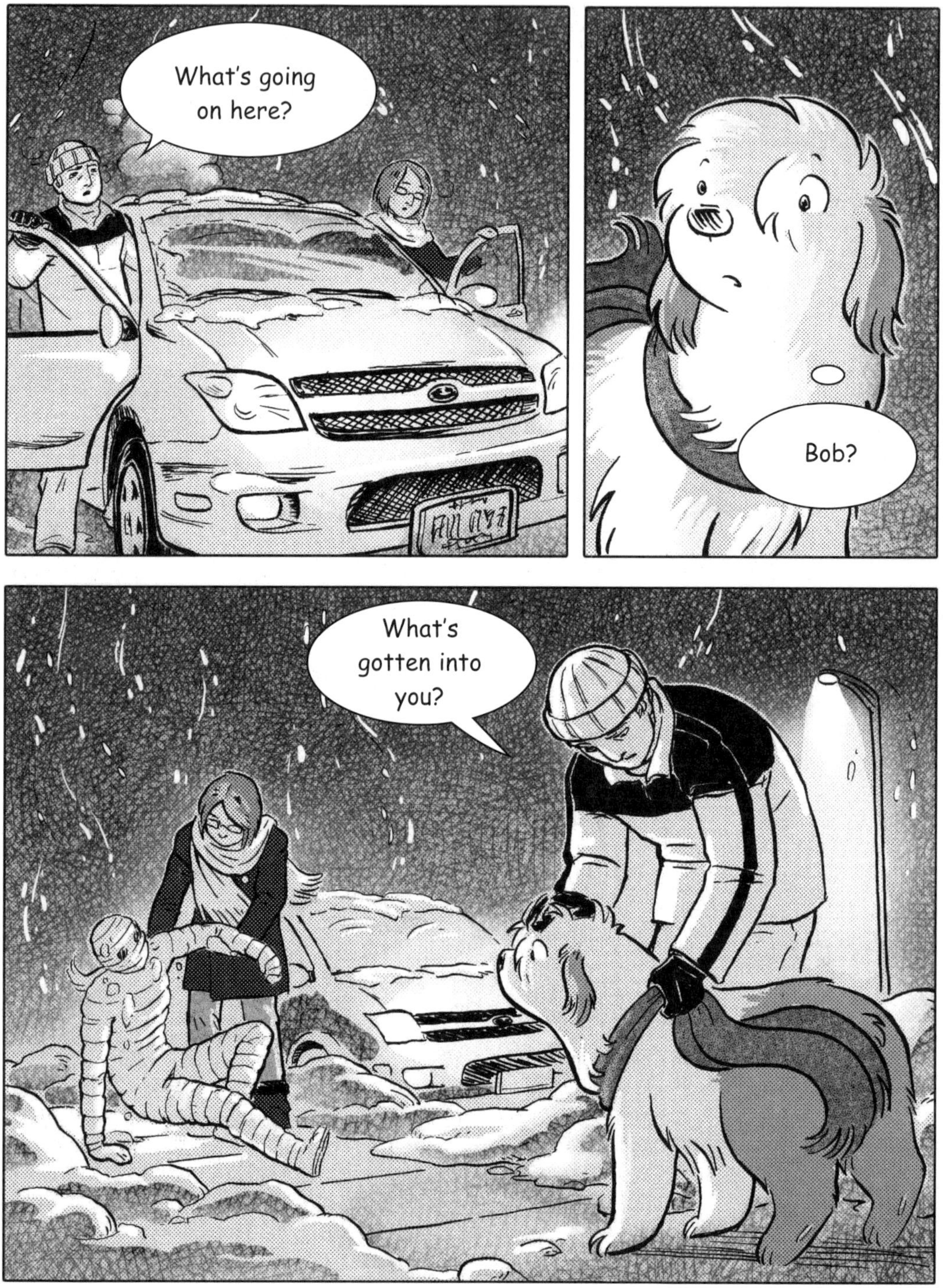
What's going on here?
Bob?
What's gotten into you?

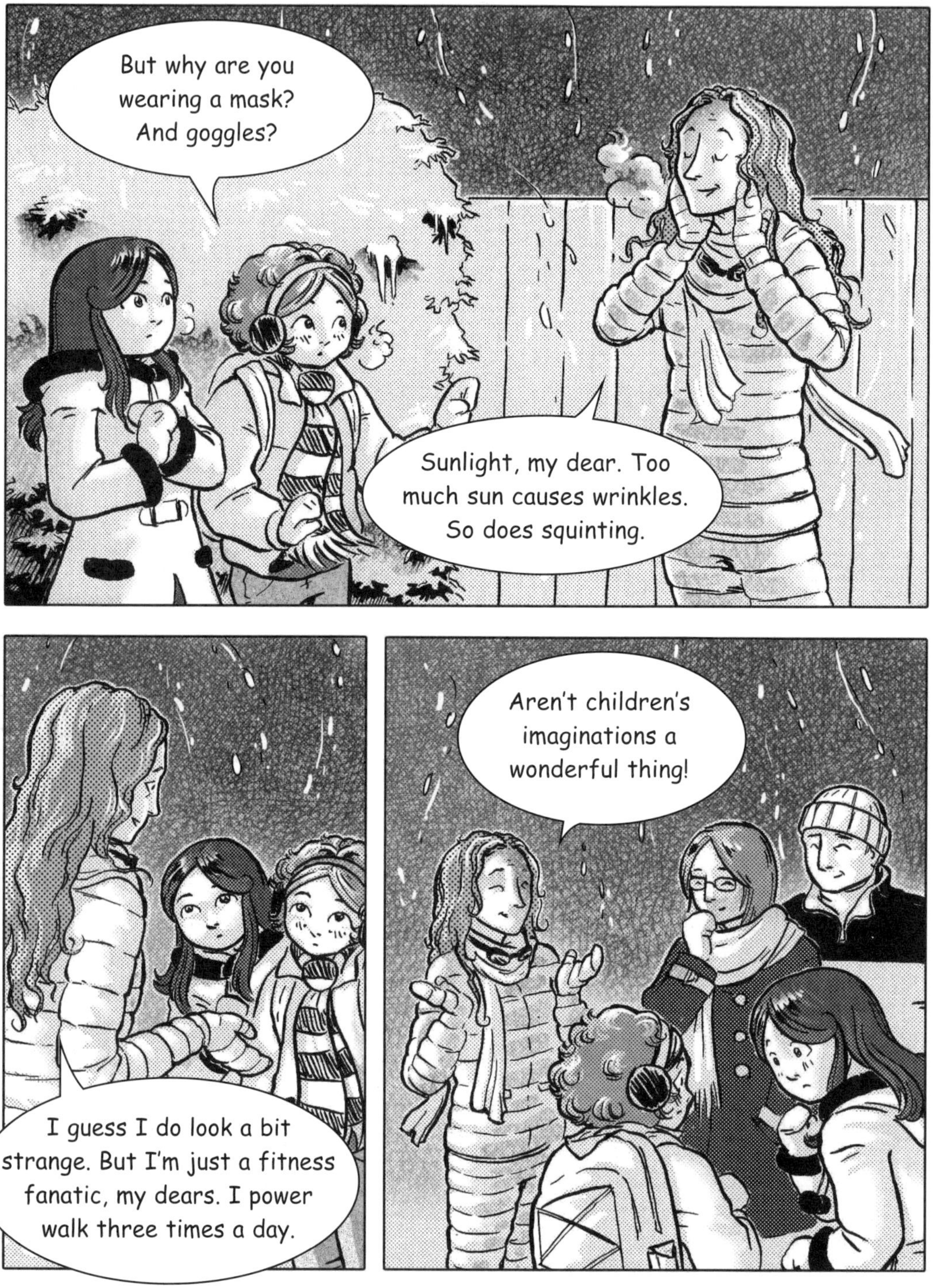
But why are you wearing a mask? And goggles?
Sunlight, my dear. Too much sun causes wrinkles. So does squinting.
I guess I do look a bit strange. But I'm just a fitness fanatic, my dears. I power walk three times a day.
Aren't children's imaginations a wonderful thing!

93

Join Claire and her friends for action-packed fun!

Claire and the Bakery Thief

Claire, her dog, Bongo, and her best friend, Jet, must catch the Bakery Thief — a recipe for fun and adventure.
Written and illustrated by Janice Poon

Hardcover 978-1-55453-286-5
Paperback 978-1-55453-245-2

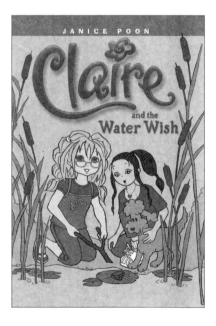

Claire and the Water Wish

After Claire and Jet's friendship hits a bumpy spot, the girls need to put their differences aside to help bring the Lovesick Lake polluters to justice.
Written and illustrated by Janice Poon

Hardcover 978-1-55453-286-5
Paperback 978-1-55453-245-2